TRÍGGER

TRÍGGER

A CIRCLE OF JUSTICE NOVEL

NEW YORK TIMES AND USA TODAY BESTSELLING AUTHOR

LP DOVER

Trigger

L.P. Dover

Editor: Crimson Tide Editorial

Cover Design by: Mae I Design and Photography

Interior Design and Formatting by

www.emtippettsbookdesigns.com

To the readers: I hope you enjoy Preston as much as I enjoyed writing him.

PROLOGUE

PRESTON

"**D**ude, where the fuck are you?"

Huffing, I slammed my hand down on the kitchen counter, wishing like hell I could throw my cell against the wall and never talk to anyone again. "On my way," I growled.

Cliff sighed. "What's taking so long?"

If he only knew. It was a bad day for me. Hell, every fucking day was worse than the last. It didn't help that my father liked to call and remind me of my failure every goddamn week. "I'll be there in a minute," I snapped.

"Dude, hurry up. Emma's been asking about you. I think tonight's gonna be your night, *if* you get out of your shitty mood."

I hung up the phone and took a deep breath, my fists clenched tight to keep my hands from shaking. Sometimes I wished my friends knew about my past, so I wouldn't have to come up with bullshit excuses every time I got pissed. Cliff was my friend and we started up a band a couple of years ago, but he didn't know about my real life; neither did Emma.

When I picked up and moved from Charleston to attend college in the North Carolina Mountains, I'd left everything behind. None of the students recognized me, or put together the pieces of who I actually was. It was nice for a while, but I was living a lie. I fought the urges inside of me every single day.

Hurrying out of my apartment, I took the stairs two at a time. The smell of weed wafted past my nose. I'd give anything to smoke a blunt and forget life for a while, but it wouldn't help. I could be stoned off my ass, or in bed with random college chicks, and still not be able to forget.

The night air was so cold I pulled my hoodie over my head and started on my way through the parking lot to one of the back street shortcuts. Snow had begun to fall and by the end of the night, the ground would be covered. Since I planned on getting drunk and going home with Emma, I didn't see the need in driving my truck.

Emma Turner was one of the only girls on campus I hadn't tried to fuck. She was more to me than just some friend, or singer in my band. However, tonight I didn't give a shit. If she wanted me, I was damn well going to make sure she got it. To hell with the consequences.

The wind whipped by my ear, howling so hard it sounded

like a scream. The street wasn't lit, but that didn't bother me. I liked it that way. The bar was only a quarter of a mile away, so I hoped the silence would help my mood. The last thing I wanted was to be a dick to Emma when she didn't deserve it.

Another muffled sound caught my attention and I stopped. There were school apartments to my right, music blaring from one of the many parties going on. However, this sound had come from my left, the direction of the woods. I heard it again and my body froze. It was a woman's scream. Only someone within close distance would've heard it.

What made my blood boil were the sounds that followed. It was as if everything inside of me snapped. The urges I'd fought for so long surfaced—there was no going back. Taking off into the woods, I was nearly blinded by my rage. The sounds grew louder and it sickened me to the core.

Everything was dark, but it wasn't enough to hide what was going on. The girl's face was pushed into the ground to muffle her screams while the fucker undid his pants, her skirt lifted and underwear ripped. She fought as hard as she could, but she was no match for his size.

I needed him to suffer . . . but even more than that, I wanted him dead. Without a word, I closed the distance and grabbed him around the neck. Hauling him up, I slammed him against a tree. It felt good to hear his howls of pain.

"What the fuck?" he spat, reeking of beer.

Squeezing his neck, I bashed him against the tree, his eyes growing wide in terror. "Feel like a man now?" I growled. "It's not so fun when you're helpless, is it?"

He gasped for air. "She . . . wanted . . . it."

Teeth clenched, I squeezed harder. "You're a pathetic son of a bitch. Let me guess, she wanted it as badly as you want this." I dropped him down, long enough to grab his chin and the back of his head. Snapping his neck, I watched him collapse lifeless to the ground.

The moment stilled my breath. I hadn't known what it would feel like to kill someone, to know it was me who took their life. Out of all the emotions I could have guessed I'd experience, pure elation wouldn't have been one of them. The high that buzzed through my body felt like nothing I'd ever experienced before. There was no remorse, no guilt for what I'd done. He deserved to die, like the countless other men out there who preyed on innocent women.

The girl's whimpers brought me back. With my hood over my head, I turned to face her. Knowing I was backlit by the moon, she couldn't see my face through her tears and the dark. Her shirt was torn and she scrambled to lower her skirt.

"You're safe now," I said, helping her up by the hand. Her whole body shook and she fell into my arms, her cries echoing in my ear. I had to get away. "You need to get help. Run to the apartments and call 911. Now!"

I let her go and she took off out of the woods toward the apartments, while I raced back to mine. There was only one thing I could do. Once I was in my apartment, I grabbed the phone out of my pocket and found my father's number. He picked up by the end of the first ring.

"What's wrong, son?"

I leaned against the door, knowing my life was about to get exponentially more fucked up. "I'm ready. Just tell me what I have to do."

1

PRESTON

(Eight Years Later)

"Summer's coming. It's getting warmer every day," Linda said, setting down my plate of eggs and bacon. She was in her late sixties, with short, white hair. I don't think there was ever a morning where she didn't wear something pink.

I took a sip of my coffee. "That it is. Luckily, I don't plan on staying in town for much longer." For the past two months, I'd eaten breakfast at her and her husband's diner every morning. Boston was just one of the cities on my list. It was time to move on.

Her brows furrowed. "You moving?"

I nodded. "New York. Lots of people over there I want to . . . see."

Frowning, she filled up my coffee cup. "I hate to see you

go, young man. I'm going to miss seeing you in here every morning. Make sure to stop in again if you're ever in town."

"I will."

Once she was gone, I turned my attention to the window. The second I heard the sirens, I grinned. Others in the diner rushed to the windows, jockeying for position to see what was going on. I knew it was only a matter of time before they found his body.

The crowd grew thick with onlookers, especially when the media showed up. Linda turned on the TV so we could hear the live coverage. "Another Trigger victim . . ." That was one of the names they called me, Trigger. The others were: serial killer, murderer, vigilante, and the list went on and on. I didn't give a fuck what the people thought. I did what I had to do.

I finished my breakfast and walked up to the counter. Linda's husband came out from the kitchen and stood beside her, both of their eyes fixed on the TV. "I bet it's that serial killer again," she stated. "It's making me nervous."

Roger put his arm around her. "I'll protect you, sweetheart."

Pulling out my wallet, I placed my money on the counter. "From what I understand, the victims are all criminals. I think you'll be fine."

Linda looked at me and sighed. "He's still a killer. Only God is allowed to dole out that kind of punishment."

"True, but not everyone wants to wait for an eternity." I slid the money over to her. "Be safe out there." I walked out of the restaurant and down the street to my car. My bags were packed and I had my rifle secured in the trunk. New York was going to keep me busy for a while.

My phone rang as soon as I got onto the highway. The caller's name popped up on my dashboard, and I blew out a frustrated breath as I pressed the button to accept it. "Hello, Glenn."

Glenn Chandler was my superior and also a good friend of my father's. They'd worked together for years in the Coast Guard, until Glenn branched out and not only joined a secret group headed by the FBI, but built a multi-billion-dollar company as well. We were fully trained, lethal assassins. I never knew anything like that existed, until my father wanted me to join. I'd spent the past eight years training and working for the FBI.

"Would you like to explain what the fuck you're doing up there?" Glenn demanded.

"I'm heading to New York. My time in Boston's done."

"You're damn right it is. What the hell were you thinking? You can't keep doing this, son. If you get caught, *my* superiors will be up my ass even more so than they are right now. They want you to slow down."

Releasing a heavy sigh, I sat back in my seat. "It had to be done."

"Not like that it didn't. We have to be careful. A kill here and there is fine, but every day? It's too much. I want to kill the bastards as much as you do, but we can't risk exposing what we are. If you can't follow the rules, you're out."

I couldn't afford to be kicked out. I needed the group. Killing was an addiction I couldn't let go. It was all I had left. "I need this, Glenn. You know that."

He blew out a shaky breath. "I know, son. But I don't want to see you go down the same path your father did."

And there it was . . . the one thing I didn't want to hear. I hadn't seen my father in years. Not since he got drunk and wrapped his car around a telephone pole, paralyzing himself. Now he was a resident of Green Meadows, an assisted living facility.

"I'm not *that* stupid," I snarled.

"Now don't start that shit. You don't know how hard it was for him when your mother and sister were murdered. He blamed himself for not being there."

"Bullshit. He blamed me. It was my fault we weren't there to protect them. Why else do you think he tried to recruit me when I turned eighteen? He thought it was my duty." I'd been the one who wanted to go on that fishing trip. If it wasn't for us leaving home, they'd still be alive. That was why I left Charleston, to get away from it all.

"He wanted your support, Preston. The desire to find the man who killed your family was too much on him."

"And look where that got us. It's been thirteen years and we still don't know who the fucker is."

The line went quiet, before Glenn sighed. "I need you in Charleston."

"Fuck that. I'm going to New York."

"It's an *order*, Hale. Either you come down to Charleston, or I'll have my sons hunt you down. You know very well they'll find you."

"Fuck," I growled, slamming my hand on the steering wheel so hard the pain shot up my arm. "What the hell are you even doing down there?" Glenn's multi-billion-dollar company was in Charlotte, North Carolina. There was no reason for him to be in Charleston, other than to see my father.

"I'm here visiting your father. It's time you saw him too." *I knew it.* "But there's something else . . ."

"What's that?" I grumbled. The exit to New York City drew closer, but instead of taking it, I continued south on Interstate 95. I couldn't believe I was doing this shit.

"Your mother and sister's case is going to be reopened," he informed me.

It was as if everything around me came to a halt. Swerving to the side of the road, I slammed on the brakes, tires screeching. "What happened?" For them to reopen the case after so many years, they had to have new evidence.

Glenn cleared his throat. "There was a murder last night. I wanted to catch you before you saw it on the news."

"Go on," I snapped. My whole body shook, my hands aching to hold the cold metal of a gun between them.

"Judging by the details, I think he's the *one*."

Heart racing, I could feel the rage coursing through my body. Stepping on the gas, I hurled back onto the interstate. "On my way."

2

EMMA

Closing my eyes, I breathed in the salty sea air and smiled, propping my feet up on the wrought iron rails of the balcony connected to my room. I loved the way the waves sounded as they crashed along the shore. We'd been in Charleston for the past week, staying at one of Glenn's many homes. And I hadn't had to do a single thing other than relax, which was odd. Working for one of the richest men on the east coast had its perks, but he was interesting to say the least. I'd been under his employ for a little over eight months now.

A knock sounded on the bedroom door. Opening my eyes, I sat up straighter and turned toward the sound. "Come in," I called.

The door opened and Glenn stepped inside, his face a stony mask. I'd seen that look a million times, but could never decipher what it meant. His dark hair had more wisps of gray than it did when he'd hired me.

"Are you busy?" he asked.

I jumped out of my seat, setting my notebook on the deck table. "Of course not. Is there something I can do for you?"

He shook his head. "Not at the moment. I wanted to stop by and share our plans." He walked further into my room and looked out toward the ocean, his crisp, button-down shirt and pants perfectly pressed. I'd never seen him look normal, in something as mundane as a pair of jeans and a T-shirt. "I'm sorry for being scarce the past week. Something came up that required my attention," he said, turning his attention to me.

"No worries. I was just working on a new song."

His lip pulled into a small smile, a rare occurrence. "How's it coming along?"

I shrugged. "Okay, I guess. It's been so long since I've written one. It'll probably sound horrible."

"I very much doubt that," he added. "I've heard you sing some of your songs under your breath." Blood rushed to my face in embarrassment. "But one of the things I wanted to talk to you about is my son," he continued. "How would you feel about working for him when I retire?"

My pulse spiked and I could feel my heart pound. Wade Chandler was twenty-nine, just two years older than me, but he made me nervous. He was extremely good looking, yet serious all the time, hardly ever smiling. I'd seen so many people give into him from a single stare. Even though I'd worked for Chandler Enterprises for several months, I'd only spoken to Wade maybe three times, and that was a *'how are you doing'* type of thing.

Brows furrowed, Glenn stared at me. "Is something wrong?"

"No," I blurted with a laugh. "Are you sure he'd want to work with me? We've never really spoken to each other."

He nodded. "I know, but it was his idea to take you on. I thought I'd ask first, to see if you were interested. The money would be the same. He thought you two could get to know each other better when he arrives."

"Is he coming to Charleston?"

Glenn's phone rang and he looked down at the screen before shutting off the sound. "He'll be here tomorrow morning," he said, lifting his gaze to mine.

"All right, I can do it," I answered. "I'm always up for a challenge."

He smiled. "You'll do fine. Once he gets to know you, he won't be so . . . uptight."

"Glad to hear it."

He started to take a step back and stopped. "There's something else I wanted to tell you. I'm hosting a dinner tomorrow night and I need you to be here. Wade will be joining us, but I have another guest who'll be arriving in town later tonight as well."

"Okay," I said with a nod. "Is there anything you need me to plan for the dinner?"

He shook his head and walked to the door. "Mrs. Walker

has it handled. I do, however, need you to find a nice dress to wear. You can charge it to the company card. The Mercedes is in the garage if you want to take it." He paused at the door and glanced at me over his shoulder. "Oh, and I won't be around this evening, but Mrs. Walker will cook your dinner when you're ready."

"Thank you." I waved as he walked out the door and shut it behind him.

It wasn't the first time I had to buy an evening gown for one of his formal events, or even drive one of his expensive cars. My biggest fear was wrecking one of them, but he didn't seem to care. Fifty thousand dollars to him was like pocket change. My family hadn't had a lot of money when I was growing up, so it was strange experiencing how the other half lived.

Working for Chandler Enterprises wasn't exactly what I thought I'd do with my college degree. After graduating with a BA in creative writing, I'd moved back to Charlotte and held a job at the local newspaper. I'd done that for five years, until out of nowhere, the infamous Glenn Chandler approached me as I walked out of the office one day. He offered me three times as much to work as his assistant and write his business proposals. I couldn't pass it up.

Grabbing my brush, I ran it through my long, blonde hair before pulling it into a ponytail. It was time to shop for my dress. Mrs. Walker was in the kitchen cleaning off the counters when I entered. She was a middle-aged woman with shoulder-length, brown hair and a kind smile. Since Glenn hadn't needed my assistance as of late, I'd been helping her in the kitchen from time to time.

"Do you need anything while I'm out?" I asked her.

She looked over at me and smiled, tossing her dishrag in the sink. "No, I'm good, sweetheart. I went to the grocery store this morning."

"Okay. I'll be back this afternoon and I can help you with dinner. We should eat together, since Glenn will be gone."

Her face brightened. "I'd like that. My husband has to work late anyway. We can eat out on the terrace."

"I look forward to it." I waved goodbye and walked into the garage, where the sleek, black Mercedes sat. I cranked it up and started on my way to downtown Charleston. King Street was the place to go, so I parked in one of the first places I could find and hopped out of the car. Before I could even shut the door, my phone rang.

"Hey, Mom," I answered.

"Hey, baby. How are you?"

Shutting the car door, I locked it and hurried across the street. "Good. Just out trying to find a dress for a dinner tomorrow night."

"That sounds nice. You still liking your job?"

I laughed. "Can't complain. I'm making more money than I would anywhere else. Besides, I've basically had the whole week off, with pay. It's nice to sit on the beach and write." My mom cleared her throat nervously. "What is it?"

"You aren't—you're not sleeping with him are you?" she

asked, her voice low.

I burst out laughing. "Oh my God, I can't believe you asked that. No, I'm not sleeping with him. Eww . . . he's like a father figure to me. It's not like that, I promise."

"Okay, just making sure. It's been weighing on my mind for a while now."

"You have nothing to worry about. However, when he retires, I'll be working for his son. Now *that* will be interesting."

"Oh," she said, drawing out the word. "Yes, it will. He's an attractive man."

"With zero personality. Trust me, there'll be no mixing business with pleasure. He's coming down to Charleston tomorrow. Glenn wants us to get to know each other, since we'll be working together in the near future."

"Just be careful. The Chandler men strike me as the kind of guys who get what they want. Don't let them run all over you."

I shook my head and smiled. Glenn and Wade had always treated me with respect. "I won't, Momma. Is that all you called to say?"

She sighed. "No, it's not. I wanted to tell you to be careful down there."

"What do you mean?"

"I was walking by the break room and saw the news. A lot of the nurses were talking about a young woman around your age who was found murdered on the beach. As of right now, they don't have any leads, which means the killer's still out there. Don't go walking around at night by yourself."

Chills ran up my spine. "Did they say where she was found, or how she was killed?" I loved walking on the beach at night.

"They haven't announced the details, but she was found not far from where you're staying. I just want you to be safe."

"I will, Mom. I'm almost always with Glenn, so nobody's going to get to me."

"All right, baby. I love you. Make sure to call your father when you get a chance. You know how he likes to hear from you when you're away."

We said our goodbyes and I walked into the boutique. My safe haven no longer felt safe.

3

PRESTON

What the hell was I doing back in Charleston? It was a huge goddamn mistake. If Glenn wanted to wrangle me in, he'd fucked up. If anything, being back made everything worse. I had no intention of facing my father, not until the man who screwed up our lives was dead. All I wanted was for the guilt to go away. No matter how many rapists and child molesters I killed, nothing worked.

My sister, Cameron, had been killed by strangulation just outside of our house on the beach, while my mother died inside. There was a struggle, but she tried her best to protect my sister, only to die from a blunt head trauma. If my father and I had been home, there's a chance they could've survived. Instead, they died alone and afraid. The thought sickened me to the core.

Glenn was parked in the Sea Dunes motel parking lot, his

stare never wavering from mine when I pulled in beside him. He waved me over, so I got out of my car and joined him in the backseat while his driver stood outside. It'd been almost a year since I'd seen him last.

"You look terrible," he said, pursing his lips.

"I'm sure you would too if you drove all fucking day without stopping," I snapped.

"That's why you're going to stay at my house while you're in town. The pool house is all ready for you. And once we're done in Charleston, you're going to work for me in Charlotte. It's about time you do something with your life besides killing people."

I was about to blast off, but he held up his hand.

"Don't even think about arguing with me. I know you don't want to be here, but there's no other choice. You're the only one who can help."

I huffed. "How's that? I haven't been in this town for years."

"You're right. But I'm hoping after you see this, it'll spark your interest." There was a folder in the seat pocket in front of him. He pulled it out and handed it to me. "Grady McConnell, the chief of police here, gave me this today. He's at the scene now waiting for us. He's going to let us look around."

Bile rose up the back of my throat. Flashbacks of seeing my mother and Cameron's bodies ran rampant through my mind. I'd looked at their files a thousand times, hoping to figure out the puzzle. I didn't want this to be the same way.

The last thing I expected was to know who the victim was.

"Fuck," I hissed, staring at a picture of the bright-eyed girl I once sat beside in my high school class. Shelly Price was one of the smart ones, always concentrating on her school work. Unlike me, who cared more about sports than anything else.

From the crime scene photos, she was strangled to death . . . just like Cameron. There were no other marks on her body, except for her neck.

According to the report, she'd been raped, but it wasn't until after she died. *Sick fucker.* I slammed the file shut and closed my eyes, clenching my teeth so hard the muscles in my jaw hurt. "Why didn't you tell me who it was?" I growled, trying to slow my breathing.

Glenn's voice lowered, but I could tell he was ready to grab me if I lost control. "I thought if you found out, it'd set you off and I'd have to hunt you down. If this is the same guy who murdered your sister, then she's the key. I need you to dig deeper."

"How?"

His gaze softened. "You need to go home, Preston. Search that house until you've combed every square inch. Something's been missed and it needs to be found."

The car felt smaller by the minute. I had to get the fuck out of there. "Forget it."

Jerking the door open, I stormed outside and slammed it shut. There was no way in hell I was going back to my childhood home. I had no clue what the place even looked like now that my father didn't live there anymore. It was probably falling apart.

The wind had picked up and the rotten decay of death surrounded me. Everywhere I went, it was all around me. Across the street, the waves crashed on the beach and there was a glow of lights where the police were investigating the scene of the crime. I wasn't the police, just a killer who worked for the FBI. I doled out punishment—just the way I liked it.

A door slammed behind me and Glenn's footsteps approached. "This could be your chance to end this, son. I know there's more to you than mindless killing. Open yourself up. Use that potential your father always told me about." His arm brushed against mine as we stared out at the dark, crashing waters. "He misses you, Preston."

"Does he know about Shelly?"

An audible sigh escaped his lips. "Yes. When he found out, he was chomping at the bit to help."

I could only imagine the pain and anger he must be feeling. I'd have killed myself if I was stuck in a wheelchair for the rest of my life.

Glenn placed a hand on my shoulder. "If he knows you're here and that you're helping, it'll make a world of difference. He'll feel like he's a part of it."

"I can't. Not yet."

"It's your choice. I'm sure you'll make the right decision." He patted my shoulder and started across the road. "Now come on."

I followed him to where the crime scene was marked off

with yellow tape. The only way to get through this mess was to shut myself off. But that'd be easy. I'd done it so much, I didn't even know who I was anymore.

Every time I closed my eyes to sleep, I saw visions of the people my targets had tortured. The smiling faces of kids who would never know what it was like to be innocent again, or the women who would always be looking over their shoulders for the next attacker. It was an endless dream I couldn't control. The only time it got better was when I killed.

Drenched in sweat, I glanced over at the bedside clock. It was three in the fucking morning. Even being in Glenn's pool house, with probably the most comfortable bed I'd ever sat on, going back to sleep would still be impossible. Unless . . .

My computer bag sat on the floor, beckoning me to open it. It was like a beacon, silently telling me it was time. It was the longest I'd ever gone without finding a target.

"Fuck it," I grumbled low.

Grabbing a clean black shirt from my bag, I put it on and reached for my computer. I turned on my laptop and felt the adrenaline coursing through my veins. There was a special government software only my group had access to. It gave us the names and addresses of possible targets, including their everyday activities. We could see which ones were eliminated and by who. Wade Chandler, Glenn's oldest son, and I were neck and neck on most kills, but I had him beat by two. Well, three, after tonight.

Scrolling down the list, my whole body shook in anticipation. It shouldn't make someone happy to kill another being, but I craved it. Grinning wide, I found a target in North Charleston. Jim Butler was right up my alley. He'd served time in prison for raping his step-daughter, damaging her so bad she wouldn't be able to have children when she got older. Most of the time, men like that didn't survive prison, but the fucker must've had luck on his side. He sure as hell wasn't going to survive me.

Grabbing my gun, I holstered it at my hip, pocketing two extra magazines for good measure. Glenn better not even think about trying to stop me. Taking my car keys, I clutched them in my hand and stormed out of the pool house. There were no lights on in the main house, but as soon as I walked past the pool, a light blared to life.

I turned to face the window, only to find Glenn staring at me. We faced off. I dared him to come out and stop me. Instead, he turned his head and shut off the light. He thought I needed to be saved, but I didn't need saving.

Jim's house was pitch black, and there was an old, beat-up truck in the driveway. Slipping around to the back of the house, I pried open the lock to the patio door and crept inside. Everything smelled like garbage and piss. The fucker snored so loud it led me right to his bedroom. He was by himself, sleeping on his back, with a hand behind his head as if he hadn't a care in the world.

I kicked his bed and he jerked awake, his hands wiping at his face. "Wha—what's going on?"

"Rise and shine, cocksucker. That must be how you stayed alive in prison . . . sucking dick."

"Who are you?" he shouted, scrambling off the bed and backing against the wall. Only, he didn't get far enough.

I pointed my gun straight at his cock and fired. His screams were deafening, and all I could do was smile as he flailed around on the floor, bleeding from his groin. He scrambled and clawed himself to the corner of the room, his face a mask of sheer terror.

Good. I wanted him to feel fear, to know what it was like to be terrified. No amount of torture was going to take away what he did. But at least his victims would know he died a horrible death. His step-daughter was the only one documented, but men like him had to hurt others; it was what they lived for.

Butler looked up at me as I towered over him, pointing my gun at his head. "Please," he begged, his body shaking.

Hearing that word infuriated the fuck out of me. There was no room for mercy. He didn't deserve it. Finger on the trigger, I glared down at him. "This is for Milly."

4

EMMA

Glenn didn't need me again this morning, so I grabbed my notepad and walked across the street to White Point Garden. Just last night, I'd watched a couple get married in the white gazebo in the middle of the park. It made me realize that was never going to be me. I didn't have time for men, other than Glenn and my father.

I walked up to the gazebo and sat down, enjoying the breeze. Summer was already here, and once July came, it'd be so hot you could barely breathe. Although, it'd definitely be better than Charlotte. Maybe I could convince Glenn he needed to work out of Wyoming for the summer. That way, we could escape the dreaded heat.

My phone rang so I set down my pad and reached for it inside my bag. I couldn't help but smile. "Look who it is," I said, chuckling as I answered the phone.

Andrea giggled. "I know, I know. I should've called you back ages ago."

"Yes, you should've, but I understand. You're a married woman now. How the hell are you?"

"Tired," she said with a sigh. "But the school year's almost up, so I'll have a nice long summer."

"Must be nice to have that kind of time off. Not that I'm complaining. The money is nice where I work."

"I'm sure it is," she replied slyly. "You happen to be working for one of the highest paid men in the country. I like telling the women at work I'm best friends with a celebrity."

I scoffed. "Please. I'm just an assistant who goes with him everywhere. Nobody knows who I am."

"But you said you don't do much for him, except write his proposals and follow him around. Most assistants answer the phone, get coffee, and all that other bullshit."

It was true. Glenn never had me do his errands. He had other people for that. "I don't know, Andy. The whole situation is strange, but I'm not gonna argue. I get to see the world and enjoy doing it. At least, I have time to write."

"True."

In the background, I heard Cliff's voice. "Put her on the speakerphone so I can say hey."

Andrea snickered. "Okay. Emma, you mind?"

"Not at all."

Cliff and Andrea were my best friends since college. I'd had others, but they either transferred or left without a trace.

She pressed the button and Cliff shouted. "Emma! What's up, babe?"

I couldn't help but laugh. "Sitting in Charleston, enjoying the weather. My boss has pretty much let me have the whole week off."

"Nice. Well, you need to come up here and visit, especially in another six months."

"Cliff!" Andrea scolded. "We were going to tell her together."

Excitement bubbled in my chest. I had a feeling I already knew what was going on. "What is it?" I asked happily.

"We're pregnant!" they called out at the same time.

"Aww . . . guys, that's awesome. Congratulations. I will definitely make it a priority to get up there. I can't wait to see my niece or nephew." Cliff and Andrea were like family. I was an only child, so being an honorary aunt was going to be exciting. I just hated that they moved all the way up to Maine. It wasn't like I could drive to see them anytime I wanted.

"We can't wait to see you," Andrea gushed. "I miss our late night talks. Plus, it'll be around Christmas when the baby's due. We can celebrate the holidays together."

"Yes, definitely. I can't wait."

We said our goodbyes and I hung up the phone. I missed my family and friends more than anything. Being able to travel was nice, but I was mostly alone.

"Emma," a deep, smooth voice called out.

Chills ran down my arms and my pulse spiked. I wasn't

expecting to see him so soon. What was he doing out here? I turned and watched Wade Chandler walk toward me, dressed in a white button-down and gray pants.

"Mr. Chandler," I blurted, getting to my feet. Running my hands over my ponytail, I could feel the knots from where the wind blew my hair.

Wade climbed the stairs to the gazebo, his posture tall and straight. "You can call me Wade," he said. I nodded and smiled, hoping my nervousness didn't show through. "My father told me you were out here. I hope you don't mind."

He had dark hair like Glenn, but his eyes were a bright blue, whereas Glenn's were green. He had three other brothers, who all shared the same looks and build, but they didn't work for Chandler Enterprises.

"No, not at all. I see you got into town safely. Traffic wasn't bad, was it?" I asked, trying to make small talk. I hated silence in a conversation. If we were going to work together twenty-four-seven, we had to be able to talk to each other.

He leaned against the gazebo, his posture slowly relaxing. "There was a bit in Columbia, but nothing more than that."

"That's good."

His gaze landed on the notepad. "What are you working on?"

Shrugging, I felt the heat rise to my cheeks. "Songs. I dabble in song-writing when I have time. I figured since your dad hadn't needed me here recently, I'd give it a go again." I looked up at him and he actually smiled.

"That sounds interesting. I love a good song. What kind do you write?"

He was definitely winning points with me. Maybe he wouldn't be so bad to work for. "Mainly pop rock. I was in a band in college. Always thought we'd make it to the big time, but that didn't happen." Clearing my throat, I picked up the notebook. "I guess we should probably head back and get ready for dinner, huh? Your father said there's someone else joining us tonight?"

Wade nodded. "A friend of the family. Why don't I walk you back and we can talk on the way?"

"Sounds good."

Wade's arm brushed against mine as we made our way across the street. "My father tells me he brought up the idea of you working for me when he hands the company over."

I nodded. "He did."

"Is that something you'd be interested in?"

"Of course." I made eye contact. "I said as much to your father."

"Yes, I know. But I wanted to hear it from you," he stated, keeping his eyes on mine. We stopped on the sidewalk and I faced him.

"Did you not believe him?" I asked with a laugh.

His gaze narrowed as if he was trying to figure me out. "I didn't think you'd agree to it. My father and I are two different men, Emma. Things might be a little more complicated working for me."

"You have nothing to worry about, as far as I'm concerned. I can handle a challenge."

His lip tilted up slightly in an amused smile. "I look forward to seeing you in action. How about we grab some drinks after dinner? It'll give us a chance to get to know each other."

"Okay," I agreed with a nod. "But I must warn you . . . there's nothing exciting to learn about me."

We crossed the street to Glenn's house and he opened the front gate. "For some reason, I don't believe that's true. There's more to you than you think."

I slipped on my brand new, silky blue dress and checked my hair and makeup in the mirror. Normally, I wouldn't care about the way I looked so much, but I had to keep up appearances since I was employed by the Chandler's. They wouldn't exactly want me parading around in yoga pants like I did before I started working for them.

Opening my bedroom door, I could already smell the meal Mrs. Walker was making. Hopefully, I wouldn't spill food on my dress and look like an idiot. I had a habit of dropping food on my clothes. Cliff and Andrea used to laugh at me all the time when we'd go out because I'd always have to make a trip back to the dorms to change.

When I got downstairs to the dining room, Glenn and Wade were already there, speaking to each other in hushed tones by the large window. There were shiny plates on the table, with all sorts of silverware around them. Start from the outside and work your way in, was what I was told when it came to using the various forks and spoons. Give me just one of each and I'd be happy.

It wasn't long before Glenn noticed me at the door and the conversation ceased. "Emma, you look lovely tonight," he announced.

I smiled. "Thank you."

He beckoned me over to the table and Wade held out a seat for me. I sat down and he took the one on the right, while Glenn sat on my left at the head of the table. There was only one other place setting and it was across from me.

"Wine?" Glenn asked, holding up the bottle.

I nodded. "Sure."

He poured me a glass and I took a sip. It tasted like heaven, all fruity and crisp. It was so good I had to take another sip, and another, while we waited on the special guest. Not even a minute later, the dining room door opened and a man walked in. Only, he wasn't just anyone.

It'd been eight years and he'd surely changed, but there was no mistaking those gray eyes. His hair was the same light brown, and mussed up like all the guys did their hair these days. However, his body looked totally different. His cream colored, long-sleeve sweater hugged a set of muscular arms, and his face was more rugged, covered in a five o'clock shadow.

I almost choked on my wine. "Oh my God." *Is it really him?*

"Emma, are you okay?" Wade asked, his voice low.

"Yeah," I whispered. "I'm fine."

I waited for Preston to look at the table, and when his gaze finally caught mine, he paused for a slight second. In his face, I could see the friend I lost so long ago, but it vanished quickly.

Glenn and Wade both stood when Preston approached, and I shot up out of my seat, bumping the table with my jerky movements. Glenn grinned at me and then at Preston. "Preston Hale, I'd like you to meet Emma Turner. She's my assistant. Emma, this is Preston Hale, a close family friend. His father is one of my dearest friends."

Preston held out his hand and looked at me as if he'd never laid eyes on me before. "It's nice to meet you."

Was he being serious? I shook his hand and made sure to put a little extra squeeze in there for good measure. "*Meet* me? Surely, you remember who I am."

Glenn's eyes went wide. "Wait. You two already know each other?"

I nodded. "From college." I was about to add *before he up and left without a trace*, but thought better of it.

Glenn chuckled and smacked a hand on Preston's shoulder. "Well, isn't this a small world? You'll have to tell me some stories on this one." He nodded my way.

Preston's jaw clenched. "Can't. Don't remember her."

My mouth dropped open; it was like being punched in the gut and slapped in the face, all at the same time. No words would come out, so I sat there with a lump in my throat. In college, he'd been a close friend. I sang with him in his band,

Silent Break. We connected on stage in a way I'd never felt with anyone. I cared about him, and had even been ready to take the next step in our relationship right before he up and disappeared. I never got to tell him how I felt. Now he looked at me as if I was a stranger.

The room fell silent. I wanted to say something, but I bit my tongue. It was going to be the longest dinner of my life.

Glenn and Wade spent most of the dinner talking, while Preston joined in with a few grunts here and there. What the hell happened to him? He wasn't the same twenty-year-old who liked to smile and have fun. Granted, he was never the happy-go-lucky type, but he was at least friendly. There were many nights where we stayed up late and talked about anything and everything. That was the guy I missed.

Once dinner was finished, Preston left the table, disappearing through the patio doors and onto the back porch. "Emma, you all right?" Glenn asked.

I plastered on a fake smile. "Of course. Why wouldn't I be?"

His gaze narrowed. "Come now, I know you better than that. It's obvious Preston's presence made you uncomfortable."

I snorted. "I guess I thought he'd remember me. We used to be good friends. I'm just baffled at this point."

Taking a sip of his whiskey, he stared at me over the rim of the glass. "Why don't you go out and talk to him?"

I glanced over at Wade and he nodded toward the patio door. We were supposed to grab drinks together. "Go. I'll come get you in a few minutes," he said.

Taking a deep breath, I slid out of my chair and walked to the patio doors. It was dark outside, so I couldn't see anything because of the lights inside the dining room. I opened the door and shut it behind me, the wind making my dress flutter. Preston wasn't on the deck, and I couldn't hear him anywhere.

Pulling out my phone, I texted Andrea.

> **Me: You will not believe who showed up in Charleston. Preston Hale.**

> **Me: Get this, the asshole says he doesn't remember me.**

> **Andrea: Oh wow! Where's he been? You sure he's not joking?**

> **Me: Nope. I don't know where he's been. He's changed.**

> **Andrea: What the hell? That's insane.**

Frustrated, I sat down on the wooden swing and huffed. "Fucking prick."

"Been called worse," Preston announced, appearing around the side of the house.

I shot up out of the swing and gasped. "Jesus, you scared the piss out of me."

There was no smile on his face as he climbed the stairs to the patio. "Sorry." Instead of stopping, he went straight toward the door, turning his back on me.

My blood boiled. "Really? That's how you're going to play this, after all these years? No, 'Hey, how ya been?' I—I can't believe this shit."

He paused and glanced at me over his shoulder, his expression unreadable.

"Why are you doing this? I was worried about you. You disappeared from our lives." For the longest time, I'd wondered if he was dead. He'd left no trace, no reason for leaving.

He looked like he was about to speak, but then Wade opened the patio door, nodding at Preston before settling his gaze on mine. "Ready to go?" he asked.

I glared at Preston, waiting on him to say anything, but I was met with silence. "Yep. I could use a drink about now." Storming past him, I didn't attempt to look back. If he didn't want to remember me, then so be it. Maybe it was time I forgot about him.

5

PRESTON

What the fuck of all fucks was Emma Turner doing with the Chandler's? I didn't think my time in Charleston could get any worse, but I was wrong. She was a distraction; one I didn't need. I watched how Wade was with her when they got back to the house after their night of drinks. He was too close. I tried to ignore the burning in my gut, but it was there. It was a feeling I hadn't had in a long time.

All I had to do was keep up the charade until I could get the hell out of town. The sun started to come up so I got out of bed and made coffee. I was too on edge to sleep. As soon as I sat down at the kitchen table, I glanced out the glass door and watched Glenn march over.

The door to the pool house opened and he charged in, his face a stony mask. "You're letting your anger get the better of you." He slammed the newspaper on the table. I didn't have to look at the headline to know what he was referring to. "You can't be doing this shit. It's sloppy. Make the kill and get out. No more, no less."

Now that Jim Butler was dead, the authorities were going straight to the people who hated him. The police were investigating Milly's mother, but I knew for a fact they weren't going to do anything about it. It was so the world would think they were doing something, when actually, they didn't give a fuck. Butler wasn't worth the time.

I drank the last of my coffee and looked at him. "The bastard deserved to feel pain. I couldn't give him the mercy of a quick kill."

Glenn's jaw clenched. "But you run the risk of exposing us. What if you were caught? My head would be on the chopping block if I let you screw this up."

"That's not gonna happen. I'm good at what I do."

He scoffed. "That's what's scary. You're worse than Wade. At least he's smart enough to enjoy life while he has it. You need to take some time for yourself."

I threw my hands in the air. "To do what exactly? Play golf? Relax by the pool? That shit's useless to me. There's too much that needs to get done."

"There are others in the team," he snapped. "They're all working on the list. No matter how many criminals you kill, there will always be more. You're not gonna get them all."

Fire burned in my stomach. "I can try."

Sighing, he took a seat at the table. "I didn't want to do

this, but you're leaving me no choice. Starting today, you're done until I give you permission. I have other projects that'll keep you busy in the meantime."

Heart racing, I slammed my hand down on the table. "You can't stop me, Glenn. I have to do this." It was an addiction. If I stopped, there was no telling what I'd do.

He stared down at me. "I can try," he said, throwing my words back at me before storming to the door.

My whole body shook with rage. I wasn't going to let him deter me.

Stopping in his tracks, he faced me again. "Wade's in the basement working out. You might want to join him. He'll tell you what you need to know. Right now, I'm going to visit your father. Might want to consider going with me before we head back to Charlotte."

He left before I could get the final word in, just like Emma had done to me the night before. Rummaging through my bag, I grabbed a pair of gym shorts and changed. A few jabs at the punching bag was exactly what I needed.

Walking through the main house to get to the basement, I opened the back patio door and Emma was right there. She walked past me without a single word. *Good.* If she was pissed at me, it made my life a hell of a lot easier. I found the door to the basement and walked down the stairs to an open room filled with top of the line exercising equipment.

Wade was on the bench lifting weights, but he noticed me through the reflection in the mirror that lined the back wall.

"Ready to get to work, Hale?"

"Depends. What do you mean by *work*?" I marched over to the punching bag and pounded away.

Wade set his weights down and walked over, grasping the punching bag while I hit it. My knuckles were on fire, but I kept going. I wanted to feel the pain; it let me know I wasn't completely numb.

"My father needs your help this week. Chandler Enterprises is expanding into a new industry and we need your help. Apparently, you have experience in this line of work."

Brows furrowed, I stopped and stared at him. "What the hell are you talking about?"

A mischievous leer spread across his face. "You're going into the music business, brother. Found out you had a band back in college." *For fuck's sake.* "We could use your help with finding some musicians here in Charleston. That is, if you don't want to audition yourself."

Sweat pouring down my face, I angrily wiped it off. "You've got to be shitting me. Did Emma tell you?"

His brows lifted. "I thought you didn't know her."

"I don't," I growled, realizing my slip.

He sighed. "No, it wasn't her. Although, we did have a nice evening. And don't worry, your name never came up."

"It's not good business to sleep with your assistant," I said through clenched teeth.

He let go of the punching bag and walked back over to the weight bench. "What Emma and I do is our own business."

Laying down on the bench, he looked over at me. "And for your information, it was your father who told us about the band. He thinks it'll help you."

"Whatever, Chandler." I grabbed a towel from the rack before heading toward the stairs. "I don't need help."

6

EMMA

If Preston was going to ignore me, the least I could do was pretend it didn't bother me. When he came up from the basement and walked through the kitchen, I busied myself on my phone until the back door opened and shut. Looking to make sure he was gone, I turned to Mrs. Walker. "Do you need any help with breakfast?"

She waved me off and laughed. "Sweetheart, no. I've been doing this for years. I can cook with my eyes closed. Thank you though."

"You're welcome. But I'm right here if you need me." I was going to miss her when we went back to Charlotte. Glenn employed different people everywhere we went. The newspaper was on the kitchen table and my stomach dropped when I saw yet another murder in the area. "Mrs. Walker, did you see this?"

She turned around, squinting from across the room to see the article. "I did. Crazy, isn't it? But that nasty man deserved to die after what he did to his stepdaughter. I doubt anyone's shedding a tear over him."

My stomach rolled while reading about the physical and emotional abuse he put his stepdaughter through. She would be seventeen right now, carrying around a burden she'd never be able to live without.

"What kind of person would do something like that?" I whispered, tears burning my eyes. Sliding the newspaper away, I couldn't stomach any more. Wade walked in, showered up and already dressed to perfection. "Good morning," I said.

He nodded once and gave me a small smile. Even though we went out for drinks, he never let on that he wanted something from me—keeping it professional. I liked that about him. At first, I was worried he'd try to come onto me. That wasn't the way I wanted to start working for him.

He poured himself a cup of coffee and joined me at the table, only he didn't sit down. "Good morning. I wanted to tell you I'm heading back to Charlotte today. When you return to the office, we'll start working together more."

"Sounds great. I look forward to it."

Mrs. Walker wrapped up an egg and bacon sandwich and handed it to him. "Be safe going home. You need to visit more. I miss you and your brothers."

He looked at her and his gaze softened. "I will. Tell Clayton I owe him a game of golf."

Mrs. Walker kissed his cheek. "Will do, sweetheart. You take care."

"You do the same." Then he glanced down at me. "See you back in Charlotte."

"Okay," I replied with a nod.

Once he was gone, I stood and grabbed a plate from the counter so I could load it with eggs, bacon, and toast. As soon as I sat down to take my first bite, Preston walked through the back door. I didn't dare look at him, so I kept my focus on my plate until he turned his back to me. He fixed a plate of food and started back toward the door, but then Glenn came in.

"Wait," he commanded, staring right at Preston.

The muscles in Preston's jaw ticked, but he turned around slowly. "Can I help you?"

"Yes, you can. Take a seat."

I'd never heard Glenn sound so demanding before. He looked angry and I hoped it wasn't because of me. Preston stood frozen in place, then huffed and stormed over to the table, setting down his plate with a loud clank.

"Did Wade tell you what you'll be doing today?" Glenn asked me. His gaze shifted to Preston when I shook my head, then came back to me. "I'm sure you remember talking about expanding Chandler Enterprises, right?"

"Of course. But you never told me what you were going to do," I said.

"You're right, I didn't. I wanted to make sure I had everything in place before I announced it." He nodded over at Preston. "This is where he comes into the picture." Preston's eyes widened, his expression appalled. "We're expanding into the music industry. And since this guy has experience in the art, I'm putting him in charge. There are five auditions today and I need you both to work together. See if any of them are good enough to receive representation."

And just like that, I lost my appetite. The blood rushed from my face and I probably looked like a ghost.

"Are we done here?" Preston snapped impatiently.

Glenn nodded once. "Yep. Be ready in an hour. George will drive you and Emma to the theater."

Grabbing his plate, Preston walked out the door and back to the pool house. Glenn watched him go, wearing a look of sadness I'd never seen before.

"Please don't make me work with him," I pleaded, trying to process what just happened. "I can get along with just about anybody, but not him. He's changed."

His brows furrowed. "What happened between you two? I'm just wondering why he'd say he doesn't know you when you say otherwise."

I shrugged. "I don't know. One day, our band is practicing new songs, and the next, he up and disappears. Do you know where he's been the past few years? I've tried looking him up, but always come up empty."

His focus was on the pool house. "That's because you won't find anything. He's had a hard life, Emma. I'm hoping he'll come around. All I ask is that you please do this for me."

I didn't want to, but I couldn't say no. "Okay," I gave in. "I'll get ready to go."

After I finished breakfast, I hurried to my room to change into a pair of dress pants and a pink, silky top. When I walked downstairs, Preston waited by the front door, dressed in dark jeans and a light blue, fitted T-shirt. Other than his shitty demeanor, he was still one of the sexiest men I'd ever met.

"I'm ready," I called out.

Preston's gaze scanned down my body, but then he opened the door and walked out. Clenching my teeth, I begrudgingly followed behind him. Glenn's driver, George, stood by the car. He reminded me of the older guy in *Men in Black*. George opened the car door and we both slid in, but I made sure to sit as far away from Preston as humanly possible.

Once on the way, I kept my focus on the road until my phone rang. I pulled it out of my purse and saw Andrea's name pop up on the screen. "Hey," I answered.

"Hey, you never called me. Tell me what's going on. What's Preston's deal?"

I glanced over at him but he didn't acknowledge me. "Do you mind if I call you back later? I'm on my way to listen to some bands play. My boss wants to dabble in the music industry."

"Oh my God, that's awesome. It's a shame you and Cliff never joined up with another band."

"I know," I said low. "But it is what it is." I often wondered what it'd be like to travel the world and sing. For a time, I thought it was possible. Preston was an amazing guitarist and singer.

"All right. Call me back when you get a chance."

We hung up and I slipped the phone back into my purse. "That was Andrea, by the way," I said, knowing he wouldn't look at me. "Not that you care, but Cliff and Andrea got married last year. They're expecting a baby."

"Good for them," he grumbled.

The man was impossible. "Did you fall and hit your head or something? Or were you always a super mega douche and I was too stupid to see it?" More like too in love with him. Back in college, I never let on that I had feelings for him. I'd tried to keep my distance, especially since he was always with someone else. The girls loved him.

His head turned and he stared at me, eyes cold. "I'm not here to hold hands and skip down memory lane. Let's just do what we gotta do and be done."

"Fine," I said, shifting to look out the window. I couldn't stand to look at him anymore.

We arrived at the local arts theater and I hurried out of the car, not even waiting on George to open the door. The building was ancient, and according to the history books, it was the first theater ever to hit the Americas. It had been renovated a few times, but nothing took away from the architecture. You could look at it and tell it was built a long time ago, a classic beauty. I couldn't wait to go inside.

There was a lady standing by the entrance and she waved when I walked up. "Hi, you must be Ms. Turner," she greeted, holding out her hand. "I'm Miranda. Mr. Chandler told me you'd be arriving with Mr. Hale."

Smiling, I shook her hand. "It's good to meet you."

Preston stopped by my side, and wasn't a complete dick, taking her outstretched hand.

"The bands are all ready for you," she explained. "I'm going to show you inside and then leave you to it."

"Great, thanks." I followed her inside and breathed in the smell of the theater. It was amazing to think our ancestors from hundreds of years ago might have been in the same building. That was what I loved about Charleston—the history. I'd been dying to take one of the ghost tours I'd heard so much about.

Miranda handed us a stack of papers that had each band's information on it. "I'll be in the back if you need me. The bands were told to play one song, unless you prefer to hear more."

"Thank you," I said. When she hurried toward the back of the theater and took a seat, I turned to Preston. "You could pretend to look somewhat interested," I growled low.

Not waiting on an answer, I marched to the front row and took a seat, while he chose to sit a couple spots away. Since it was his job to find the talent, I waited on him to acknowledge the band, but he didn't. *Cocksucker.*

"Good morning," I announced. "Please, begin when you're ready."

The lead singer looked back at his band and nodded before staring down at me. "We're First Sanity, and the song we're going to play is called Summer. It's one of our biggest hits."

The second the guitar played, I was sucked back to a time eight years before. It reminded me of what it was like to belong to a group. I could almost see myself up on stage with Preston and Cliff, auditioning for opportunities like this.

A smile lit up my face and I closed my eyes. I didn't realize how much I'd missed it.

Once we arrived back at Glenn's house, Preston went straight through the side gate, no doubt to hole up in the pool house. Glenn was in the living room with a tumbler full of whiskey.

"How did it go?" he asked, sounding hopeful.

I set my purse on the couch. "The bands were great. I just wish I had a little input from my partner."

His lips pursed. "He didn't help, did he?"

"Not at all. In fact, he was a downright ass, refusing to acknowledge the bands, or me for that matter. Please tell me I don't have to work with him anymore. I didn't sign on for this."

Sighing, he tossed back his liquor. "I know, but I need your help. Just give it another week."

"A *week*?" I gasped incredulously. I couldn't handle another day.

Glenn stared right into my eyes, his features morphing.

There was something about Preston that made him a different man—a man steeped in grief. "Please, Emma. All I ask is that you work with him for another week. There are more bands scheduled to play for the next few days, and then again on Monday and Tuesday of next week. Once Wednesday comes, you can head back to Charlotte."

"I'm starting to think I should ask for double time having to put up with him. As a side note, he won't make it to next week if he keeps up with this attitude. I will kill him first."

A mischievous smile spread across his face. "You're more than welcome to smack him around a few times. You won't get fired if you do."

Now that made me laugh. "It's a serious possibility." But then I sighed in defeat. "All right, I'll stay. But it's not something I want to do."

"Thank you, Emma. Just take notes on the bands you like, and what you like about them. I trust your opinion."

That meant a lot coming from one of the most successful men in the country. "If you trust my opinion, why does Preston have to be there?"

His gaze shifted over to the window and out to the pool house. "I'm sorry, you'll have to trust me on this." He blew out a heavy breath and grabbed his suitcase from the floor.

"Are you leaving?" Surely, he wasn't going to leave me alone with Preston.

Glenn glanced down at his bag and then over at me. "I'm needed in Charlotte. I have no doubt you'll be okay here by yourself. Mrs. Walker will cook your meals and you're more than welcome to drive one of my cars."

Dread settled into the pit of my stomach. It was going to be one of the worst weeks of my life. "Now I really need that double time pay."

He chuckled. "It's already been applied."

Mouth gaping, I watched him walk out the front door. Well, damn . . . I should've asked for triple pay.

7

PRESTON

Grabbing my car keys the next morning, I opened the front door of the pool house and walked out, only to run into the one woman I wanted to avoid.

"Hey," she gasped, tucking a strand of blonde hair behind her ear. She was dressed in a white skirt and a light blue top.

Clenching my teeth, the last thing I needed was to look at her long, tanned legs. But dammit to hell, I couldn't stop. There'd been a time when I'd wanted those legs wrapped around my waist as I fucked her. "What do you want?" I snapped.

Her face immediately soured. "And here I was trying to be nice." Huffing, she nodded toward the front of the house. "It's time to go. We have more auditions to listen to."

I scoffed. "Correction. *You* have more auditions to listen to. I have other plans."

Throwing her hands in the air, she walked away. "Have

it your way, douchebag. Works better for me anyway. Now I don't have to look at your face for the rest of the day."

The girl was going to fucking kill me. She walked off and there was no denying how unbelievably sexy she was. Her hips swayed back and forth, reminding me of how I hadn't had sex in weeks. I could use a good fuck, but I didn't have time. As soon as I did what I had to do, it was back to my computer to find my next target.

The drive to Isle of Palms wasn't backed up with traffic like it usually was in the summer. Once school was out, it'd be that way soon enough. I hated being there when it was packed with people. My old childhood home was off the main strip of the island, just a quarter mile down from where Shelly's body was found. We always had a lot more privacy than some of the other places. And in the end, it was one of the main reasons nobody came to my mother's rescue; she wasn't heard.

It'd been seven years since I'd last visited the place. My father couldn't bring himself to sell it, even though he never stepped foot back into it once the investigation was complete. We'd combed that place from top to bottom and never found anything. No clues as to who the killer was.

When I arrived at my house, you could tell it'd been neglected. The yellow siding was more like a light brown, and some of the shrubs had grown across the stairs leading up to the door. It was one of the smallest houses on the island, but we had the best stretch of coastline all to ourselves. We never worried about swarms of people taking up our beach.

I looked up at the house and released a shaky breath. I'd spent years trying to make up for the loss of my mother and sister, but nothing worked. They were gone, no matter how many people I killed.

Taking the wooden steps two at a time, I reached a small piece of yellow crime scene tape still stuck to the railing, and my gut clenched. Everything from that night flashed through my mind.

I remembered walking through the door and seeing my mother's lifeless body on the living room floor, her chocolate-colored hair matted down with dried blood. My father's screams still echoed in my ears as he rushed over to check on her. It was a sound I never wanted to hear again.

Searching through my keys, I found the one for the front door and opened it. The smell of dust hit me, but was overpowered by the stench of death. I knew it was my own mind playing tricks on me, but it didn't keep me from staring at the spot where my mother had died.

Walking around the room, there was a thick layer of dust on everything. Nothing had been moved. I looked out the window at the swimming pool and there was nothing in it but a couple feet of dirty water and sand. What I wanted to avoid seeing most was the spot on the beach where my sister had been found. Her death would always be a puzzle to me. The thought of what happened to her made me goddamned sick to my stomach.

Closing my eyes, I turned away from the window and

stormed up the stairs. My parents' room was the same as it'd always been. And across the hall, Cameron's door was shut. I stared at it, trying to remember if I'd shut it last time I was there. My hands shook and I could feel the rage inside my chest, aching to let loose. The door handle was cold as I grasped it, a sinking feeling washing over me. Something wasn't right.

I opened the door slowly, my heart thundering in my chest. Once I looked in her room, I realized why I had that sinking feeling in my gut. "Fuck," I growled. Everything in her drawers and closet were thrown across the room, as if someone had been searching for something. "Son of a bitch."

Nothing in the house was turned upside down, except for her room. I didn't like that at all. Pulling out my phone, I called Glenn.

"Shouldn't you be at the auditions?" he asked.

"Fuck that. We have bigger problems."

"What is it? Is Emma okay?"

"Yeah, she's fine. I'm at my old house. Cameron's room is ransacked. I think someone was looking for something. Nothing else in the house was touched."

"What the hell? How did they break in?"

I rushed down the stairs to the back door and it was locked, sealed perfectly. What the fuck was going on? All of the windows were secure, and there was nothing that'd suggest a break in. "There's no evidence of tampering. The front door was locked and the same goes for the back door and all of the windows. Whoever it was must've had a key."

"Holy shit, this changes things, Preston. If the same killer is back in town and has a key to your house, then the murder was personal. We need to go back to the beginning." Which meant seeking out Cameron's close friends. "Just do me a favor and keep this under wraps. If the fucker finds we're onto him, he might run. With Shelly being found just a few short days ago, he's probably still around."

Rage consumed me. "Got it. I know what to do."

8

EMMA

had an hour before I needed to be at the theater, so I stopped at one of my new favorite cafés down the street. It had the *best* blueberry scones and hot chocolate. Once I got my order, I sat down at one of the small, white tables and blew the steam off my hot chocolate. I was glad I got in before the morning rush.

Reading the newspaper on the table beside me, I caught a headline about a woman's body being found on the beach. She'd been my age. And still no leads as to who the killer was. Scary. If anyone tried to hurt me, I'd fight until my last breath.

"Good morning, Ms. Turner," a voice called out.

Gasping, I jerked my head up, almost knocking over my hot chocolate. John laughed and steadied my cup before sitting down in front of me. He had sandy, blond hair shaved close to his head, and a wide smile, which I didn't see often on men. It was refreshing.

"Didn't mean to scare you. I saw you sitting here and thought I'd come over and say hey."

"Hey," I echoed, moving the newspaper out of the way. "How are you?"

John Tallman was the lead singer and guitarist for First Sanity, one of my top three choices from the auditions. Setting his coffee down, he smiled. "Doing good. Just getting ready to head into work. I like to stop here in the mornings to get my coffee."

"Work? I thought you played for a living?"

He shrugged. "It pays the bills, but it's not enough yet. The guys and I are hoping to change that one day. Right now, I work at the aquarium."

That was when I noticed the aquarium logo on his green polo shirt. "Sounds like fun. Do you get to feed the fish?"

Chuckling, he took a sip of his coffee. "That and clean the tanks."

"I'll have to stop by." I might as well. I didn't have anything else to do, since Preston basically left me on my own.

"I'll be happy to show you around. How long are you in town for?" he asked.

"Til next Wednesday, then I'm heading back to Charlotte. I have a few more bands to consider."

Clearing his throat, he glanced down at his coffee. "Have you and your partner made any decisions yet?"

I snorted. Preston had completely distanced himself the

past two days. I kept trying to tell myself it didn't bother me, but it did. Especially when he'd leave late at night and not come back until dawn. I couldn't help but wonder where he went. "His opinion doesn't matter to me. I'll be making the decision on my own. But I can say that your band is one of my favorites. It reminds me of the one I used to be in many years ago."

His face lit up. "You were in a band?"

"Is it so hard to believe?" I laughed.

He shook his head. "Not at all. Did you play or sing?"

"Both," I confessed. "I play the keyboard. It was an amazing feeling being on stage."

"What happened? Why aren't you in one now?"

I thought back to that time and how heartbroken I was when Preston left. "The leader of our band left, and we never quite recovered."

His gaze softened. "I'm sorry to hear that. I don't know what I'd do if I didn't have my band."

"Just hold on to it for as long as you can."

"I plan on it." He looked down at his phone and sighed. "I should probably get going. Don't want to be late for work." His gaze shifted to my left, then back to me, before doing it again. When his brows furrowed, I turned and looked behind me. There was nothing there.

"Everything okay?" I asked.

"Do you have a boyfriend, or a husband?" His gaze shifted to my left hand.

"No, why?"

He nodded toward the door. "There was a guy outside who couldn't stop staring at you. He was over by the tree. But when he saw me notice him, he walked away."

I jerked my attention to the windows again. "Really? What did he look like?"

"Couldn't tell," he replied. "But he looked around our age."

"Was it my partner?"

He shrugged. "Don't know. I never paid much attention to him the other day."

Goose bumps flittered across my arms and up my neck. "That's strange. Maybe this guy thought he knew me."

"Don't know. Seemed kind of weird though," he said, getting to his feet. "Just be careful. Do you want me to walk you to your car?"

I took another bite of my scone and waved him off. "I'll be fine. Go, before you're late for work. I'll call you with my decision early next week."

He smiled again. "I look forward to it."

Once he was gone, I finished my scone and hot chocolate, keeping my gaze on the tree just outside the window. If Preston was following me, we were going to have some serious problems. I wasn't about to put up with it.

I looked down at my phone. There was still thirty minutes before I had to be at the theater. Making a split decision, I got up and headed home.

Preston's black sports car was in the driveway. Storming past the side gate, I circled around to the pool house. The blinds were open on all the windows, and I could see him walking around inside before sitting down with his back to me at the kitchen table. Instead of knocking, I slammed open the door.

Clearly knowing it was me, he didn't even bother turning around. "Can I help you?" he asked.

The man was seriously going to drive me insane. "Yeah, you can stop following me around."

"And why would I be doing that?"

"Hell if I know. You've been skulking around all hours of the night, so there's no telling. Maybe you get off on it. Who the fuck knows. But I'll let you know—right fucking now—I don't like being watched."

He jerked around, eyes blazing as he shot up out of the chair. "What do you mean *being watched*?"

His reaction wasn't what I expected. Instead of anger, like I'd seen for days, there was concern in his gray eyes. Holding up my hands, I backed away. It was best to just stay away from him. "I don't have time to deal with this shit right now. Consider yourself warned." Turning on my heel, I hurried off.

"Emma!" he shouted after me, but I couldn't be bothered to stop.

If it wasn't him watching me . . . then who was it?

9

PRESTON

It was nine o'clock and I knew she wouldn't be done at the theater until two. I had plenty of time to do what I needed to do and then meet her there to make sure she got back okay. She wasn't going to like it, but I didn't give a shit. The only person who could follow her around was me . . . and it hadn't been me earlier this morning.

After searching for my sister's best friend, Lainey McGee, on the internet, I found all of her information. She was now an accountant in Mt. Pleasant, only a short drive away, and married to a Dillon Walsh.

Picking up my phone, I called her office. I hadn't seen her since I left home for college.

"Hello, Lainey Walsh," she answered.

I closed my eyes, clenching my teeth hard. "Lainey, it's Preston, Cameron's brother." She gasped and the line went quiet. "I need to talk to you."

"Jesus Christ, Preston. I haven't seen or heard about you in years. How are you?"

"Not good." There was no reason to lie. "We need to talk. I have some questions I need to ask you."

"O-okay," she stuttered uneasily. "I'm here until three. If you want, you can come here."

"Be there in twenty." I hung up and got in my car.

It didn't take long to get there, and when I arrived, she was outside by her car. The short, red hair she'd had before was now long, and she was pregnant. Years back, I remembered listening to her and Cameron talk about how they were going to get married at the same time and have kids together. It was what they'd planned all their lives.

Lainey's eyes went wide when she saw me get out of my car. She slapped a hand to her mouth and walked toward me, her arms outstretched. "It's so good to see you," she cried, trying to hug me. Her stomach got in the way, so it ended up being more of a pat on the shoulders.

She wiped tears from under her eyes. "How's your dad doing?" she asked.

I shrugged, not interested in talking about my father. "Don't know. Just got into town. I need to ask you some questions about Cameron though." Her lips trembled and she rubbed her stomach like she was in pain. *Great.* The last thing I needed was for her to have her baby because I stressed her out. "Are you okay?"

She blew out a shaky breath and nodded. "I'm fine. Been having contractions. What all do you want to know?" Her watery gaze looked up at me.

"Do you know if Cameron ever gave anyone a key to our house?"

With pursed lips, she shook her head. "Not that I know of. Unless she gave one to Adam. Why do you ask?" Adam Payne had been Cameron's boyfriend of five years, up until she was killed. She grabbed my arm. "You don't think he did something, do you?"

Adam had been playing in a football game at Duke the night she was killed. He was never even a suspect. "No," I answered truthfully. "Someone broke into the house recently, and ransacked Cameron's room. They had to have gotten in by key."

She slapped a hand over her mouth. "Oh no. What were they looking for?"

"I don't know, but I was hoping you'd have some ideas. Do you know if Cam hid anything in her room? Like secret things she didn't want anyone to find?"

Lainey shrugged. "We all did stuff like that. I know she had a diary. Where she kept it, I have no clue."

If she had a diary, all I had to do was find it. In order to do that, I had to go back. "Thanks, Lainey. I'm sorry I had to come to you like this."

Her lips trembled as she smiled. "It was good to see you, Preston. You and Cameron have the same eyes. It's like I can see her in them."

Chest tightening, I turned on my heel. "Take care of yourself, Lainey. Congrats on the baby."

"I'm naming her Cameron," she called out. I paused and glanced over my shoulder. Lainey rubbed her stomach and smiled at me.

"Cam would've liked that," was all I could say. I had to get out of there. Hopping in my car, I sped away, hands shaking. The pain triggered the need to kill. Eventually, I'd find the fucker who murdered my sister and mother, but until then, I had to do what needed to be done.

Once I was back at the pool house, I ripped open my laptop and logged onto the *list*. There were countless targets all over the fucking country. Until the day I died, I would go after them. It just so happened there was a target a couple hours away, in Myrtle Beach.

But first, I had to make sure Emma was safe.

She walked out of the theater at two o'clock, with a smile on her face. She loved music. I knew it from the very beginning, back when I first met her in college. It was why I agreed to let her sing with me.

Her smile disappeared the second she saw me standing by her car. "What are you doing here?" Her face turned red, nostrils flaring. She was sexy as hell when she was pissed.

I blocked her from getting into her car. "I wanted to make

sure you got back to Glenn's safely."

She scoffed. "Why do you care? Get out of my way."

"I'm not going anywhere until you listen to me," I said, standing firm. I looked into her bright green eyes, something I'd tried to avoid since being around her. Once I had her attention, I continued, "It wasn't me who was watching you earlier."

Her face paled and she froze. "If it wasn't you, then who was it?"

"I don't know, but it's best you not wander around the city alone."

She snorted. "Please, Mary Poppins, I've done just fine on my own for years. It's not like I need a nanny, I know how to take care of myself. Besides, aren't you the one who left me alone the last few days?"

Narrowing my gaze, I crossed my arms over my chest. "It was a mistake. It won't happen again."

Her scowl turned into a leer and she laughed, but I could see the pain in her eyes. "Don't you get it? I don't want you around. I'm just here to do my job until next Wednesday, when I can go home, and hopefully never see you again." We stared at each other for the longest time, but she broke contact first. "Can you please move out of the way? I'd like to get back."

Knowing she was about to break down, I stepped out of the way so she could get in the car. "I'll follow you home."

Glenn's car roared to life and she sped away before I could get back in mine. It wasn't hard to keep up with her, and when we arrived, she bolted inside. I followed behind her, giving her the distance she needed. It didn't surprise me when she slammed the door to her bedroom.

"My goodness," Mrs. Walker called out, hurrying from the kitchen. She looked at me, then up the stairs. "Is everything okay?"

I shrugged. "I'm used to people being pissed at me."

She grinned. "Something tells me you bring it on yourself. Don't worry, she'll get over it. I've seen the way she looks at you."

"With what, disgust?"

"No." She chuckled with a wave of her hand. "She cares about you. But I have to say, you're going about it all wrong."

"Trust me, it's for the best."

"Suit yourself." She turned to head back into the kitchen, her voice echoing down the hall. "If you were my husband, I'd have beaten you silly by now." I'd have done a lot worse than that if I was Emma. "Do you want me to bring your dinner out to the pool house?"

I sat down on the couch and flipped the TV on. "Nah, I'll be eating in here tonight." I needed to make sure Emma was safe in bed, before I left.

10

EMMA

The wind picked up and a sheet of gray clouds moved in across the horizon. We were about to get a nasty storm. I could smell the rain approaching as I sat on the balcony. Thankfully, it wasn't hurricane season.

Scouring through my notepad, I finally landed on one from my past. It was one Preston and I wrote together but never got a chance to perform. Seeing it reminded me of the place we'd go to in Boone, where we'd picnic and just get away. It was the place we'd go to think up new songs. And before he disappeared, we'd spent the day there, writing this particular song.

Thinking about how he acted this afternoon, I wondered what in the hell was going on? One minute, Preston was a gigantic ass and now he was trying to keep me safe? It was like I was in a twilight zone.

I mean, in college he used to be overprotective, never letting me walk around campus at night by myself, but I understood the reasoning. There were too many incidents where girls were attacked, and some even raped. But now, he was just being ridiculous. We weren't in college anymore. Hell, I didn't even know him anymore.

A soft knock sounded on the door to my room. When I opened it, Mrs. Walker was there, her gentle smiling face a breath of fresh air.

"Hey. Sorry for slamming the door earlier," I apologized.

She waved me off. "No worries, sweetheart. If I had to deal with that man, I'd have done the same thing."

"Is he still down there?" I asked, whispering the words.

She nodded. "He is. I believe he wants to eat dinner with you."

"No," I hissed low. "Is there any way to bring my food up here? Please."

A mischievous smile spread across her face. "Of course. He deserves it." Turning on her heel, she disappeared down the hall. Coming back quickly, she handed me a tray of food and it smelled heavenly. There was meatloaf, mashed potatoes, green beans, and a homemade biscuit.

"Thank you so much," I gushed, breathing in the aroma.

"You're welcome, sweetheart." She nodded toward the stairs. "I don't think the young man downstairs is happy about you eating up here."

I scoffed. "He can get over it."

"Well, you enjoy and I'll see you in the morning." Her gaze shifted to the window. "Hopefully the rain will let up." She smiled again before heading toward the stairs.

I shut the door and locked it before setting my tray on the bed. Instead of watching TV while I ate, I watched the rain. It reminded me of the time Preston and I got stuck in the rain on a hiking trip all those years ago. It was the first and only time we'd ever kissed.

Hours passed and after a long phone call with Andrea, the time had closed in on ten o'clock. Everything was silent downstairs, but I had yet to hear Preston leave . . . which meant he was still inside. I refrained from turning on the TV, for fear he'd come up the stairs and I wouldn't hear him. I wanted to be prepared.

However, nothing could prepare me for Preston Hale. His footsteps thumped up the hardwood stairs and down the hall to my room. My door was locked, but that didn't stop him from twisting the knob. I held in my gasp and jumped in bed, pulling the covers as close to my face as possible.

A light knock sounded on the door. "Emma," he called out, his voice dark yet soft. He knocked again. "Emma, let me in."

I wasn't about to get up. He turned the knob and it rattled. I smiled triumphantly, but that changed when the hallway light shone into my room. *No!* How'd he get in? Closing my eyes, I laid still and slowed my breathing. His steps drew near and my heart raced. What the hell was he doing in my room?

He stopped at the edge of the bed and I realized I'd left my notepad wide open. Our song was there, in plain sight. The last thing I wanted him to think was that I still cared about him. The sound of the paper rustled and I bit my cheek. *Fuck my life.* His steps quickly retreated and the door shut gently behind him.

Sitting up, I tiptoed to the door, pressing my ear to it. He was setting the alarm. Little beeps sounded before the front door shut. It was a good thing I knew how to turn it off. Slipping on my shoes, I rushed downstairs and peeked out of one of the kitchen windows. There were lights on in the pool house, but then Preston emerged, carrying a bag in his hand— not even caring that he was being drenched by the rain.

He disappeared around the side of the house and I hurried to the living room so I could watch him get in his car. It was then I got a good look at what he had strapped to his side . . . it was a gun. What the hell was he doing with a gun?

Once in his car, he slowly backed out of the driveway. Grabbing my purse and the keys to Glenn's car, I turned off the alarm and locked the door behind me. I had no clue if I was going to catch up to him, but I had to try. If he wasn't going to tell me where he was sneaking off to, I would find out myself.

Luckily, the rain made people drive slowly and I was able to see him up ahead, stopped at a traffic light. As soon as we hopped on US-17 North, I had a feeling we were headed to Myrtle Beach. Why would he want to go there so late?

Two hours later, we arrived in Myrtle Beach. I hadn't been there in years, not since I was a little girl and it was the prime spot for vacations. There were at least eight cars between me and Preston, but it didn't look like he knew I was behind him. However, when he turned into the parking lot of a questionable bar, I rode past, trying my best to blend in with the other cars.

Out of all the bars in Charleston, why would he choose one in Myrtle Beach? Especially one littered with violent drunks, judging by the fight going on in the parking lot. There was nothing around but an old warehouse, dark alleys, and a twenty-four-hour diner across the street. Not a place I'd go to by myself.

I parked at the diner and watched him go inside the club. A part of me hoped like hell he wasn't going in there to meet another woman, but then the other part wondered why I even cared. I didn't want to care, but something inside me couldn't let go.

The clock ticked away and my eyes grew heavy. I should've stayed in bed. The two-hour drive back was going to be torture. Several people stumbled out of the bar and went to their cars, while others walked across the street toward the diner. It wasn't long before Preston came out. Instead of going to his car, he followed a man heading toward the side of the rundown warehouse.

Was he going to buy drugs? With his complete attitude and personality change, it wouldn't surprise me. I was either stupid, insane, or both, but I was determined to see what he'd been up to these past few nights. Rummaging through the glove compartment, I found Glenn's gun. He had them in all of his cars. It was a good thing my dad taught me how to shoot.

Getting out of the car, I slipped the pistol into the back of my jeans and ran across the street. I could see Preston's shadow against the side of the warehouse wall. Adrenaline coursed through my veins, my steps silent against the pavement. The alley was disgusting, with trash everywhere, and it smelled ungodly. It was the kind of place you'd find a dead body in.

"Who the fuck are you?" the man shouted.

"You should've known I'd come for you the moment you got out of jail." The sound of Preston's voice made me shiver; it didn't sound like him.

Peeking around the corner, the only thing I could see was Preston's back and the man in front of him, holding up his hands, staring down the barrel of a gun. I held a hand over my mouth to keep from making a sound. The man looked angry, his beady eyes blazing. Preston pulled the trigger and there was no sound, other than the thud of the bullet passing through the man's skull. Blood splattered across the side of the building and that was all I could take.

"Oh my God. Oh my God," I repeated over and over, speeding onto the highway. I couldn't get away fast enough. Preston *killed* someone, in cold blood. He was a murderer. There was no way in hell I was going to stay anywhere near him.

Pulling out my phone, I pressed Glenn's number. I didn't give a rat's ass if it was two in the morning. Glenn picked up, his voice sounding as if he was still awake. "Emma, are you okay?"

"No," I shouted, on the verge of tears. I was too keyed up to cry, but I knew it'd happen as soon as the adrenaline wore off. "When I get back to Charleston, I'm packing my shit and leaving. I'll return your car to you tomorrow."

"Whoa, slow down and breathe," he soothed. "Now tell me what happened."

Visions of what I saw flashed through my mind. It felt like I was going to throw up, but I swallowed it down. "I can't, Glenn. I just can't," was all I could say. I hung up and shut off my phone. I didn't want to talk to him or anyone else about it. That wasn't the Preston I knew. Or maybe it was, I just didn't know.

The two hours passed by quickly and once I got to the house, I reset the alarm. If Preston was going to come looking for me, I wanted a warning. Sweat poured down my face as I raced back and forth to get my stuff packed. The sound of the alarm going off, stopped me in my tracks. And when the alarm went silent, my pulse doubled. There was someone in the house. I could hear them moving around.

Reaching for my phone to call the police, I realized I'd left it in the car along with the gun. *Shit!* The only thing in my room that could be used as a weapon was one of the fireplace pokers. Nabbing it, I walked out of my bedroom and down the stairs. I wasn't about to sit around and wait for them to come find me.

And since I hadn't turned on any lights in my rush to get the hell out of there, the entire downstairs was dark. I moved into the living room and a hand grabbed my arm. I swung the poker as hard as I could and screamed as it connected with flesh, only the shout that came out of the man's mouth was *not* Preston's voice.

"Fuck me," he growled, stepping away. I didn't recognize his voice at all, so I panicked even more when another man came up behind me, holding me in his vice-like grip.

"Drop the poker, Emma," he said, whose voice sounded almost familiar.

I wanted to fight, but I couldn't move. "Who are you?"

The man I hit walked over to the light switch and turned them on. My eyes adjusted to the light and I thought I was going to be sick. Another man walked in and I dropped the poker in shock. He was someone I did recognize.

"Oh my God," I cried.

He nodded toward the door. "It's time to go."

11

PRESTON

I didn't know what I'd been thinking breaking into Emma's room, but I sure as hell never expected to find the song we'd written together. I hadn't played my guitar or sang in years.

Seeing her notepad frightened me, and my plan on telling her I never forgot her, our friends, or our band, flew out the window. Instead, I hunted a target. Now that was what I knew how to do.

After making the kill, I drove back to Charleston and watched the sunrise. I didn't even try to sleep, knowing I'd dream of her, of what could've been. It wasn't easy seeing her in that bed alone. It made me wonder how many men had had the privilege of being with her, of having her legs wrapped around them.

"Fuck," I hissed, pacing the pool house. I wanted her and I couldn't get her out of my goddamn head.

A quick knock jerked my attention to the door. Mrs. Walker hurried in, her breath coming in rapid pants. "Is Emma in here with you?"

"No, why?" She was panicked and I didn't like it.

She waved for me to follow her. "Looks like there was a scuffle in the living room involving an iron poker. There's blood on the floor. I'm thinking Emma used it on her attacker."

"Are you fucking kidding me? Have you called the police?" My chest tightened and I rushed past her. Fear flooded my veins; something I hadn't felt in a long time.

"I wanted to make sure she wasn't with you," she cried. "I tried calling Glenn, but he's not answering. And we can't call Emma because her phone's in Glenn's car."

I took the stairs two at a time. I knew I shouldn't have left her alone. If her phone was in her car, there was no way I could track her without it taking forever and a goddamned day. When I got to her room, I wasn't expecting to find her bedroom lights on, and all of her clothes stacked beside a suitcase. Where was she going?

My hands shook when I pulled my phone out to call Glenn, only to realize I'd missed several calls from him.

"Make it quick, son. I'm in an important meeting," he answered, sounding slightly annoyed.

"I don't give a shit what you're doing. Emma's gone," I growled. The sinking feeling in my gut grew worse each second she was gone. Whoever took her wouldn't live long once I got my hands on them.

"Yes, I know. She was upset last night when she called. What'd you do to her?"

That took me completely off guard. "What did *I* do to her? Not a fucking thing. What was she upset about?"

"I don't know. She said she was leaving and would return my car to me today. I figured she'd be here by now, giving me her resignation. I tried calling you to see what happened, but you obviously had better things to do."

"I was doing my job," I stormed. "But it doesn't look like she left willingly. Someone broke in and took her."

"What are you talking about?"

"Just like I fucking said. Someone broke in and took her. Why didn't the alarm go off?" I could feel my resolve slipping. Images ran rampant through my mind—Emma beaten, raped, and left for dead in an alley. I had to find her.

"I don't know. But you have to calm down."

"Fuck calm! She's gone!" I ran back to the pool house to grab my guns and knives. It was time for a hunt. I strapped my knives to my belt and holstered my guns before charging toward the driveway. Glenn's car was unlocked and I took her phone out from the center console.

"Where did you go last night? You should've been there to protect her," he snapped.

Frozen, I stared at Emma's phone, at the picture of her, Andrea, and Cliff. I knew where I was last night. I'd chosen to kill instead of protect. The guilt I harbored inside my soul came back with a vengeance. *We should've been there to protect them*, was what my father said to me all those years ago.

My chest felt like it was going to rip apart, the rage too much to contain. I glared at the front door, the place where Emma was no doubt dragged out, screaming and frightened. Then up in the corner there was a flashing, red light.

"I'll find her," I barked.

Through the phone, I heard a car door slam. "I'm on my way back to Charleston. I'll call my friends at the PD to get a search on her."

I tore inside the house. "I'm not waiting. Where's the security footage? It has to show something."

"In my office, there's a hidden door that leads to the media room. I have no doubt you'll see it. Everything should be in there."

Heart racing, I ran to his office and spotted the hidden door. It blended in with the wall, but the difference of texture was easy to find. Inside, there were six different TV's, all displaying different areas of the house. However, none of them showed anything from the inside. *Fuck.* There was no way to see if Emma was hurt.

I put the call on speakerphone and set it down.

"Seeing anything yet?" he asked.

Once in the system, I turned back the feed to the night before. I saw myself leave, knowing damn well I set the alarm on the way out. Then it wasn't two minutes later when Emma walked out the front door and got in her car.

"Fuck me," I hissed.

"What is it?"

She drove away and disappeared down the street. "Emma left last night. I checked on her before I left and she was sound asleep." Obviously, she hadn't been. Where the hell was she going?

"She called me around two in the morning. Search the feed around that time."

I did as he said and fast forwarded the footage. It was right after two when she pulled into the driveway and ran up to the front door with a look of terror on her face. My protective instincts went on full alert. Emma could be a pain in the ass, but she wasn't the scared type. It had to have been bad for her to react like that.

"Something happened. She's scared," I reported.

"If you were making a kill, shouldn't you have been back by then?" Glenn huffed.

I clenched my teeth. I should've been. "I fucked up, okay?"

About that time, a man in black circled around the side of the house. I couldn't see his face because it was hidden by a hat. A car approached, the headlights off as it pulled into the driveway.

"What the hell?"

"Tell me," Glenn demanded.

"Someone was already here, waiting on Emma before she even showed up. Then another car pulled in when she was inside." The one guy disappeared through the front door, and another one followed. Not a minute later, another man got out of the car and walked around the side of the house toward the back. "There were three of those cocksuckers," I growled.

Three against one. The thought made me so fucking sick, I couldn't see straight. Emma was a pistol, but she wouldn't have been able to fight off three of them.

"I'm getting the PD on this now. You'll need help finding her."

I watched two of the men drag her out of the house and put her in the car. As soon as they sped away, I paused the footage, getting exactly what I needed when I zoomed in on the license plate. "I don't need help," I thundered. "I know what to do."

EMMA

Nothing made sense. I wasn't hurt and I wasn't going to be, definitely not by the men who took me. Once I'd been put in the car, I was told I would not be harmed—I was being hidden for my own safety. If I'd have seen their faces through the dark, I'd have known who they were. There was no mistaking the Chandler charm. Ian, one of Glenn's other sons who happened to be my age, had taken the poker to the side of the arm, while his twin brother, Bryce, held me back from doing more damage. That was when Glenn appeared and said it was time to go. We were headed to one of his other houses.

Was I scared? Hell yeah, but not for my life. I was terrified of the unknown. That was why, the next morning, I was afraid to open the bedroom door. I didn't know if I was ready to know what was going on. Glenn said he'd give me answers first thing in the morning and it was time.

A knock sounded on the door and I froze, heart racing. I didn't want to open the door. It didn't matter because it opened anyway and Ian walked in, bare-chested and wearing a pair of running shorts, his light brown hair drenched. Ian Chandler didn't live in Charlotte like his father and Wade. All I knew about him was that he spent most of his time out west along with his brother, Bryce. His skin glistened with sweat but it was the bandage on his arm that caught my attention.

A mischievous smile spread across his face when he noticed me staring at his arm. "You know, you can always kiss it and make it better. I have no doubt you could take the pain away." His gaze roamed up and down my body and I glowered at him, crossing my arms over my chest. He burst out laughing. "Damn, Turner, I'm kidding. My father told me you're a feisty one. My brother's gonna have his hands full when you start working for him."

"After last night, I don't think I want to work for you people anymore," I said in all seriousness.

His smile faded and he sighed. "Look, I was just trying to lighten the mood. I came up here to see if you're hungry. There's food downstairs. My father will be back in a few minutes and I know he wants to talk to you."

I glanced down at the clothes I wore last night, wishing like hell I could take a shower or at least brush my teeth. Ian nodded toward the closet. "There's some clothes in there if you want to change. And there's toiletries in the bathroom."

Brows furrowed, I met his gaze. "Thanks, I think."

He winked. "I'll see you downstairs. And don't even think about trying to run away. I'll catch you before you could even get out of the house." Stopping at the door, he glanced at me over his shoulder. "We're not your enemy, Emma. Remember that," he said, shutting the door behind him.

After showering and putting on a fresh set of clothes, I took a deep breath and opened the bedroom door. Everything was quiet, except for the sound of pots and pans clanking together in the kitchen. My first thought went to Mrs. Walker. Was it her?

I tiptoed into the kitchen and it was Ian making all the noise, his back to me as he cooked. "You can sit down if you want."

"How did you know I was in here?" I asked. I hadn't made a sound as I entered the room.

He chuckled. "I know a lot of things, Emma."

There was juice on the table with a couple of empty glasses so I poured me one and took a sip; my mouth was very dry. "Why am I here?"

He scooped some eggs and bacon onto a plate and turned around, setting it right in front of me before making his own plate. He sat across from me and poured himself a glass of juice. "We need your help," he said with a sigh. "And you're the only one who can do it."

"I don't understand. What do you need me to do?"

A door shut behind me and I gasped, jerking around to see who it was. Glenn stood there, dressed in a pair of khaki pants and a white button down, his gaze sad as he stared down at me. He looked like a completely different man, not the powerhouse everyone back home saw him to be. "Finish eating and I'll tell you everything." Then he looked at Ian and said, "Outside, now."

Ian inhaled his food and hurried outside. I saw them through the window, but I couldn't hear what was being said. Ian nodded a few times and then took off around the side of the house. Glenn sat down on one of the patio chairs, his shoulders hunched over as he watched the waves.

Once I finished my food, I joined him outside, shutting the door behind me. His body stiffened but he kept his focus on the water. "I need answers, Glenn," I demanded. "Why am I here? You're supposed to be in Charlotte."

Releasing a heavy sigh, he got to his feet and faced me. "Let's take a walk. I promise I'll tell you everything, but just know, you're safe here. The last thing I want to do is scare you."

He nodded toward the beach and I followed him onto the sand. "Are you trying to keep me safe from Preston? If so, you should've thought about that in the first place when you left me alone with him."

"Preston would never hurt you," he murmured. "But I know what you saw him do. That's what scared you off."

My throat tightened and I froze. "How do you know?"

Glenn's serious, crystal green eyes met mine. "Because I had him followed. I didn't expect for you to be there too."

"Do the police have him?"

He chuckled but there was no humor in it. "No. We fight on the same side."

It felt like the breath had been knocked out of my lungs. "*We*? Does that mean you . . ." Feeling sick to my stomach, I closed my eyes and sucked in a breath.

Glenn touched my shoulder, but I was numb. "It's my job, Emma. I'm the leader of a secret FBI group that targets criminals who escaped the justice system. We're called the Circle of Justice and we're not cold-blooded killers. The man Preston killed last night had just gotten out of jail for child pornography."

He grabbed my shoulders, the fire blazing in his eyes. "The bastard pimped out his younger nieces and filmed them with older men. They were seven and nine. He deserved to die. Those girls will never get their innocence back. Preston kills men like him, to protect the people of this country."

Tears filled my eyes. I was appalled, yet grateful there were people who sought justice when the system failed. To think that kind of shit actually happened in our world made me ill. The fucker deserved to die. "So Preston is part of the FBI?"

Sighing, Glenn's hands slid off my shoulders. "Yes."

"Is that why he left all those years ago?"

"To join us, yes. He's part of the COJ. He had to go through extensive training, just like my sons."

"Your sons?" I interrupted. "Like *all* of them, including Wade?" He nodded and I felt dizzy. *I'm employed by killers.*

"Preston works for me and is one of the best assassins on

my team."

I held my stomach. "Why are you telling me this if it's top secret? I don't think I want to know."

"You have to," he said, his voice full of pain. "Preston needs your help. In order to give that to him, you have to know everything." We walked back to his house and sat down on the lounge chairs, wind whipping by. It was warm outside, but I couldn't stop shivering. I was nervous, but most of all, scared to hear what he was about to say.

Glenn focused on the horizon, so I did the same, clasping my hands together to keep them from shaking. "I worked with Preston's father in the Coast Guard many years ago and we became close friends. As a result, I think of Preston as a son. And about thirteen years ago, Preston's mother and sister were murdered when he and his father left to go on a fishing trip."

I slapped a hand to my mouth and faced him. "Oh my God. He never said anything. I asked him questions all the time, but he found ways to change the subject. I just thought he had a bad childhood."

He shook his head. "No, he had a wonderful family. But after they came home and found them dead, his father lost it. Eventually, he became an assassin and tried to recruit Preston. It wasn't until years later that he decided to join us. It was the night he saved that girl at your college from being raped. After that, it triggered something inside of him. He's never been the same since."

Closing my eyes, I fought back the tears and the pain in

my chest. No wonder Preston wasn't the same. "So that's why they never caught the guy who killed the bastard that night," I whispered, realizing it all made sense.

"And nobody ever will. Preston does his job well, but lately, he's not the same. I need to get him back before we lose him completely. That's why I hired *you*."

"What?" I gasped.

"I hired you months ago, in hopes of bringing you and Preston back together. We researched you long and hard before I sought you out."

I rubbed my hands over my face. "Holy shit, this is insane. So you lied when you said you needed someone to write your proposals?"

He shrugged. "Not exactly. You're an amazing writer, and one day you'll put that talent to use—other than silly proposals—but I had to do everything possible to get you here. You had a connection to Preston once before, and I need you to get that again. It's the only thing I can think of that might save him."

"So you knew this whole time about our past and pretended you didn't?"

"Yes," he confessed. "I didn't want Preston to know I knew about you two."

I scoffed. "I don't see how your plan's going to work. He wants nothing to do with me." If I were being honest, that wasn't exactly true, considering his behavior yesterday.

"I beg to differ. He's terrified right now, and declaring he'll find you. I have no doubt he will." Glenn's phone rang and he cleared his throat before answering. "Bryce, what's going on?" He put it on speakerphone so I could hear. The sound of horns blared in the background.

"He's getting close. What do you want me to do?"

Glenn glanced at me, then closed his eyes with a sigh. "Ditch the car. I didn't realize he'd catch on so fast."

"Will do. I'll have Ian pick me up."

They hung up and my heart raced. "What's going on?"

Glenn got to his feet. "Preston's tracking you through the rental car. Once we ditch it, he won't be able to find you."

"What happens then?" I looked up at him, my stomach a ball of nerves.

He looked down at his phone. "We wait. I have to test him, to see if he's willing to give up killing to find you. If he does, then I know he can be saved."

"And if he doesn't?"

"Let's just hope, for his sake and ours, that Plan A works."

EMMA

(One Day Later)

I couldn't sleep knowing Preston was out there searching for me. It made me wonder if Glenn's plan was actually fathomable. Looking over at the clock, it was already after midnight. I heard voices downstairs, so I got out of bed to see who it was. When I walked into the kitchen, Ian and Bryce were at the table with a deck of cards.

They looked exactly alike, except for the eyes. Bryce had a ring of gold in his blue eyes that Ian didn't have. But I could tell Ian was the jokester of the two by the mischievous smile on his face. It was strange to think that guys like them, with all the smiles and good looks, could be assassins. They weren't brooding or complete jackasses like Preston. Then again, Preston didn't used to be like that.

"Wanna play?" Ian asked, nodding toward the cards.

I sat down. "Sure. Know how to play BS?"

They both smiled while Ian shuffled the cards. "I'm a master at it." He laughed.

Bryce snorted. "What the fuck ever. He loses every time."

I wanted to laugh, in hopes it'd take my mind off the situation, but it didn't work. "Have you heard anything on Preston?" I asked.

Ian glanced over at Bryce, his expression serious. "Might as well show her."

My heart dropped. "Show me what?"

Releasing a heavy sigh, Bryce pulled out his phone. "I recorded him when he found the rental car. I can show it to you, if you want."

"Yes," I gasped, moving closer to him. "Please do."

He scrolled through his phone until he stopped at the video. When he pressed play, I thought my chest would split open. Preston's eyes were frantic as he ripped the door open, searching every inch of the car. It was the most emotion I'd seen out of him since we'd reunited.

Slamming the car door, he leaned against it, hands pulling at his hair. His chest rose and fell so rapidly, I thought he'd hyperventilate. Bryce shut off the phone.

"No! Why did you stop it?"

He met my gaze, then looked away. "Because you don't need to see anymore."

"Why? What did he do?" They both exchanged a look, as if they were trying to protect me. "Look, I'm not a scared little girl. I already know what you guys are and what you do. I watched Preston kill a man right in front of me for Christ's sake."

Bryce scoffed. "Yeah, and we all saw how well you reacted to *that*."

I rolled my eyes. "That was before I knew the reason why. If I could do what you guys do, I would in a heartbeat. I wouldn't think twice about pulling the damn trigger."

They stared at me and I stared back, unrelenting. "Fine, we'll tell you," Ian spoke up. "If there's one thing Bryce and I have learned about Preston, it's that he hates to fail. And after that video was recorded, he let his anger get the best of him."

"What did he do?" I didn't know if my heart could take anymore.

Sighing, Bryce scrolled through his phone. "Basically, he tore the car apart."

I slapped a hand over my mouth when he showed me the pictures. The windows were broken and one of the doors had been ripped off its hinges. It didn't even look like the same car. "Oh my God," I gasped.

Bryce pulled back his phone. "We've known Preston ever since we were kids. Our fathers used to take us camping. He's not the same." I remembered Preston talking favorably about the camping trips. "Ian and I have both tried to reel him back in. I can see why he's fucked up though, especially after everything that happened with his mother and sister, and now his father."

I held up my hands. "His father? Glenn never told me anything about him." I glanced back and forth between him and Ian.

Ian set down the cards and sighed. "As you'd assume, Preston's father was fucked up after the murders. He searched relentlessly for the killer, but never found him. Other than Preston, he has one of the highest kill counts on our team. Unfortunately, it got the better of him."

I was on the edge of my seat. "What happened?"

His jaw clenched. "He got drunk one night and wrapped his car around a tree. Now he's paralyzed from the chest down."

Tears fell down my cheeks. "My God. I can't imagine having to go through all of that. How can one person deal with so much loss?" It was the kind of stuff you saw in movies. No wonder Preston was shut off from the world. I would've been the same way.

The front door slammed shut and Glenn walked into the room, brows furrowed when he looked over at me. "I thought you were in bed?"

I shook my head. "Couldn't sleep."

"You okay?" he asked.

Getting to my feet, I could feel my heart pounding, my conviction strengthening. "We need to end this now."

"It's only been a day, Emma."

"I don't care. Sitting here is not going to help him. I can do this, I can bring him back."

His gaze narrowed. "You sure about that? Even after

knowing what he is?"

Did Preston's profession scare me? Hell yeah. But I also knew he'd never hurt me. All I had to do was make him remember what it was like to live and be loved. I couldn't give up. "Yes," I answered with all my heart.

"Do you have a plan in mind?"

Taking a deep breath, I glanced at the Chandler men. "How are your connections at the hospital?"

14

PRESTON

My knuckles were bloody and I didn't give a shit. I couldn't rest until I found Emma, even if I had to kill everyone who got in my way. Only now, I was fucked. My link to her was gone. The car I'd tracked down was empty, just sitting on the side of the road, not far from a rough neighborhood in North Charleston. Now I was back at Glenn's, standing at the door to the pool house. It was two in the morning, but I refused to sleep until she was safe.

I wasn't stupid though. I knew the longer she was gone, the less of a chance I'd have at finding her. I lived in fear of hearing news reports about a young woman found dead.

I had no choice but to ask for help; I was desperate. Pulling out my phone, I found Glenn's number. However, when I was about to press the button to call, he called me instead. My gut clenched and I swallowed down the bile.

"Yeah," I answered, not knowing what else to fucking say. "Where are you?"

"Searching for Emma. I won't stop until I find her."

He sighed. "She's been found, son."

Closing my eyes, I gripped the wooden rail of the deck, the wood biting into my skin. "Where is she?" I demanded. The line went quiet and everything inside me exploded. "Where the fuck is she, Glenn?"

"At the hospital in Charleston. She was found about an hour ago running down the road. She was able to escape her attackers."

I bolted to my car. "On my way," I growled before hanging up.

"You can't see her right now," Glenn said as I blazed into the waiting area, demanding access to her room. "Look at you. She's been through enough already. Get yourself cleaned up and then you can see her."

Anger boiled in my veins and my teeth clenched so tight the muscles in my jaw ached. "I *have* to see her. I need to know who did this, so I can kill them."

Glenn shook his head. "You can't. They've already been taken into custody. It was three men. Apparently, they've been watching her for days, waiting to make their move. They were going to sell her to the highest bidder."

My whole body shook with rage. "What did they do to

her?" He glanced nervously around the room, where others watched on curiously. I wanted to yell at them to mind their own fucking business.

He moved closer and lowered his voice. "They didn't violate her, son. They wanted her in good condition for when they sold her. She's a little shaken up is all. But she's strong. Not many women could escape from something like that."

I breathed a sigh of relief, but it didn't last long. I couldn't rest until I saw her. They might not have raped her, but she didn't deserve the terror they put her through. As soon as I found out who those fuckers were, they wouldn't last long on this earth.

"I need to see her, Glenn," I said in all seriousness.

A look of turmoil passed across his face. "They're running some tests, but they said she'll be free to go soon. We're keeping this under wraps for the time being. We don't want the media involved. The doctors are going to let me slip her out the back when we leave."

"What about her parents?"

He shook his head. "They don't know. She didn't want to tell them just yet. Her mom worries enough about her as it is. Right now, I want to get her out of here as fast as I can. While the police are still searching for evidence at my house, I rented another one not far away. Meet me at the back and follow us there." He marched off to the elevators and disappeared inside.

I was a failure.

I wanted to see Emma, but I didn't want to tell her I'd failed. She would never forgive me. Instead, she escaped on her own and went through it all by herself.

It wasn't long before Glenn texted saying he was sneaking Emma out the back. My car idled near the door, and I couldn't see her face as Glenn ushered her outside. There was a blanket wrapped around her, hiding her face from view.

Glenn helped her into the car and we started on our way toward the Isle of Palms. The house he'd rented was located several houses down from my childhood home. Emma got out of the car, wearing the same clothes from the night before, only now they were dirty and torn. I wasn't going to be satisfied until I killed the fuckers who took her.

She rushed inside before I could catch up to her. Glenn stopped me with a hand to my shoulder. "Give her a minute. Let her wash up and change clothes. She'll talk to you when she's ready. Maybe you should give her until morning."

That wasn't going to happen. "Okay," was all I could say.

Glenn walked off and I circled around to the back of the house. There was a light shining through the glass door on the second floor. A shadow moved past, and there was no mistaking Emma's golden blonde hair.

I jumped as high as I could, grabbing the bottom railing of the balcony. Pulling myself up, I climbed over onto the balcony. The curtains over the window were sheer and I could see into her room. Her dirty clothes were already in a pile on the floor, and a bathrobe covered her body as she reached to touch the water pouring into the shower.

I couldn't look away, especially when the robe slowly dropped to the floor, exposing her bare skin underneath. A need sparked deep inside of me. And for the first time in a long time, it wasn't the need to kill. No, this ran bone deep. I ached to touch her skin, to mark her as my own.

As soon as she stepped into the shower, I backed up against the wall. My dick was harder than a fucking rock and I palmed myself like a horny teenager, thinking about spreading her wide and plunging deep. I wouldn't be able to rest until I did. I'd never had sex with anyone I gave a fuck about. But there was something about her I couldn't ignore.

Fuck. I had to get control of myself. The last thing she needed right now was some hard-up loser creeping on her through a window. Opting to give her some space, I stayed against the wall, contemplating my next move.

Once Emma was dressed and in bed, she turned off the lights. I knew I should listen to Glenn and give her some space, but every fiber of my being told me to go in there and hold her. But I couldn't. I couldn't let myself give in. However, I also couldn't let her go without telling her the truth.

The patio door was unlocked, so without overthinking it, I snuck inside, gently shutting it behind me. Emma's breathing was light and steady, her blonde hair fanned out across the pillow. I couldn't see her face, but I could tell she was falling asleep. The last thing I wanted to do was scare her after all the shit she'd been through.

"Emma," I murmured.

She moaned and turned around, her body facing toward me. She was absolutely, fucking beautiful. I sat on the edge of the bed and started to touch her lips, when her eyes fluttered open. Before she could make a sound, I covered her mouth with my hand.

"Shh, it's just me. Don't be scared." Her body relaxed and I let her go.

She sat up and leaned against the headboard. "What are you doing in here?"

"I wanted to make sure you were okay. Glenn didn't tell me much."

Her brows furrowed. "I'm fine. But honestly, I didn't think you'd care."

I shook my head. "You have no idea. I never stopped looking for you. I couldn't rest, not knowing what was being done to you."

"It doesn't matter now," she whispered. "All that matters is that it's over and I'm safe. I don't really want to talk about it."

Eventually, she was going to have to. I had to know what they did to her; if they touched her. That way, I could make killing them that much more painful. "I should've been there to protect you."

"Just like you were in college?" she countered softly. Smiling to herself, she appeared to be reliving a memory.

"You got so pissed at me that one time, when I walked across campus at night by myself."

I didn't want to remember my past, but looking into those soft, green eyes of hers, I couldn't deny it. "And then after that, I walked with you everywhere," I added.

Her eyes lit up. "So you *do* remember? Why lie about it?"

I shrugged. "It's just easier that way."

"Easier? How? We were friends, Preston. I cared about you, and so did Andrea and Cliff. I tried looking you up for years. It gutted me when you didn't say goodbye."

"That time in our lives is over. It should stay in the past." I got off the bed and walked back to the balcony door.

"Preston, please," she begged. "Don't go. I want to understand."

I opened the door, making sure to keep my back to her. If I looked into her eyes again, I would cave to her every desire. "You won't be able to, Emma. I'm not the same guy you knew before."

15

EMMA

waited for Preston to sneak back into my room, but he never did. I felt horrible for going along with Glenn's plan. When Preston told me he never stopped searching for me, my heart dropped. I could see the pain on his face. I was deceiving him.

Since I could barely sleep, I left the balcony door open all night to feel the breeze. Once I heard movement downstairs, I changed into a pair of shorts and a T-shirt and threw my hair up in a ponytail before tiptoeing down. Now that we weren't at Glenn's main house, Preston didn't have the pool house to sleep in, which meant he was nearby.

The noise came from the kitchen and my heart raced. What was I going to say to him? It didn't matter anyway because when I turned the corner, it wasn't him. Mrs. Walker had her back to me, cooking away in front of the stove, while Glenn sat at the kitchen table, dressed in the usual suit attire.

There was a full plate of eggs, bacon and toast in front of him and my stomach growled. He lifted his cup of coffee to his lips and paused when he saw me.

"Good morning, Emma," he called out, trying to hide his mischievous smile.

Mrs. Walker jerked around, drawing my attention to her. She gasped when she saw me and hurried over, dropping her spatula on the counter. "I'm so glad you're okay," she cried, hugging me tight. "I was so worried about you. It's a good thing they caught the guys who took you."

I hugged her back, guilt ridden. "Yes, it is. But I'm fine, I promise. It's something I don't ever want to remember."

"I know, sweetheart. We don't have to talk about it if you don't want to."

"Thanks, Mrs. Walker," I said, smiling sadly. I hated I couldn't tell her the truth, and hated even more that we had to put her through the stress.

She let me go and inspected me with her motherly eyes. It was a good thing my parents didn't know anything about what I was doing. They'd have made me quit, especially if they knew I worked for trained killers. "You hungry? I made you some pancakes to go with your eggs and bacon."

My stomach growled again. "Sounds amazing. I'm starved." I sat down at the table with Glenn and she brought over my food. "Thank you," I gushed, breathing in the aroma.

She chuckled as she walked to the sink and cleaned the last of the dishes. "I'm going to head out and run my errands.

But I'll be back to cook dinner." She glanced at me over her shoulder. "Do you need me to bring you anything?"

I shook my head. "I'm good, thank you. Honestly, I just want to get back on a normal schedule."

"And that you will," Glenn added.

Mrs. Walker finished up the dishes and grabbed her car keys, her gaze concerned as she looked at me. "You sure you don't need anything? I don't like you being alone."

I glanced from her to Glenn. "I'm going to be alone today?"

Glenn sighed and smiled at Mrs. Walker. "She'll be fine, Martha. Preston will be here with her while I'm gone." She pursed her lips, but it didn't seem to faze him. Once she was gone, he blew out a breath. "If looks could kill, I'd be dead right now." He finished his coffee and sat back in his chair.

"What's going on?" I questioned.

He nodded toward the direction Mrs. Walker went. "She's upset I'm leaving town without you."

"You are?" I blurted. "Or are you pretending to, like you did before?"

"No, I'm really going this time. *You* need to stay with Preston. I know he snuck up to your room last night."

My cheeks burned. Hopefully, he didn't know I intentionally dropped my robe so Preston could see me naked. I had known he was out there watching me. "How do you know that?"

He scoffed incredulously. "Because I know him . . . and you just confirmed it." He winked. "Don't worry. It's what I was hoping for. With a little more time, I think you can get him back. That's why I want you two here for another couple of weeks."

"A couple of weeks?" I gasped.

Grabbing his cup, he got up and set it in the sink. "Preston already knows. I told him this morning before he left. There are a few more bands I want you to listen to. Pick out your top choices and call them back for a final audition. All I ask is that you take your time." He turned back around to face me. "Do whatever you have to do to get him back. His father really wants to see him. I'm stopping by now to visit him before I head back to Charlotte."

My chest ached. I couldn't imagine not seeing my father for a long period of time. "How long has it been since they've seen each other?"

"A couple of years. Preston has it in his head that his father blames him for his mother and sister's deaths. He's never stopped searching for their killer. What's crazy is I think he's back in town."

Gasping, I slapped a hand over my mouth. "You can't be serious. After all these years?" Chills ran up my spine. The thought of the killer being back was almost ludicrous. What were the odds?

He nodded. "The girl who was found last week was killed and dumped in the same vicinity of Preston's sister. She was murdered in the same manner as Cameron. In fact," he pointed out the window, "she was found not far from here, right on the beach outside from his childhood home. Preston and his family lived about a quarter mile down that way. That's where he is now."

There was an uncertainty on his face I didn't like. "What are you not telling me?"

Closing the distance, he reached out and placed his hands on my shoulders. "His house was recently broken into, and the only room that was trashed was his sister's. We think it might have been the person who killed her looking for something."

I felt sick to my stomach. "What would they be looking for after all this time?"

He shrugged. "I don't know. Maybe you can help him figure it out. He's not going to rest until he finds the fucker."

"What if he doesn't want my help?" I countered.

He squeezed my shoulders. "You're just going to have to force it on him. You're not afraid of him, like most others. I need your help to keep him grounded. He's not going to leave this place until he knows for sure this killer isn't the one who murdered his family." My body trembled and his gaze softened. "You don't have to stay, Emma. I would never ask you to do anything I didn't think you'd be able to handle. I just don't want to lose him."

About that time, Preston appeared on the beach, heading back to the house. Seeing him, I knew then I would do anything to help him, even if it meant hunting down a killer. "I won't leave him," I whispered, keeping my eyes on Preston. "You have my word."

"Is there anybody worth listening to?" Preston asked as he drove us to the theater.

It was the first words he'd spoken to me all morning. There was a tension between us and I knew he felt it too, judging by the stiffness in his shoulders. I wanted to touch him and play around like we used to. "Actually there is. I already have my top three picks in my head."

He glanced over at me, his gaze narrowed. "What's their style?"

I shrugged. "Similar to ours. A little bit alternative, with a smidge of pop rock. If only Cliff was here, I'd say we audition ourselves." His jaw tensed and he focused his gray eyes back on the road. "You were really talented, Preston. So many people thought we'd hit it big one day."

"I can't change the past, Emma," he said, his voice low.

"I know. I just thought maybe you needed to be reminded of how good you were." He scoffed, but didn't comment. "It's true. I'd give anything to hear you play again."

"I haven't picked up a guitar in years. Never have time for it."

It was about time he did. Grinning from ear to ear, I thought up the perfect plan. One way or another, I was going to get a guitar in his grasp. He looked over at me and I tried to hide my smile.

"What are you smiling for?"

"No reason," I lied, straightening my face. The café was just around the corner and I could really use another cup of their hot chocolate. I hadn't had it in days. "But I'll be super happy if you stop by that café over there." I pointed to the quaint little building with aqua colored shutters.

Preston parked on the street and sighed. "Let's go."

We walked into the café and I breathed in the scent of fresh baked bread—pure heaven. I ordered my hot chocolate and couldn't resist getting one of their blueberry scones. "Do you remember that restaurant we used to go to in college?" I asked, sitting down at one of the two seater tables by the window.

He sat back in his chair, lips pursed. "Is there nothing else you can talk about? Why do you insist on bringing up the past?"

I took a bite of my scone. "Because it's all I know of you. Plus, it was some of the happiest times of my life. It's hard not to talk about when I'm looking at you."

Moving closer, he ran his hands through his brown hair, then rested his elbows on the table. I waited for him to look into my eyes, but he didn't. He was avoiding it at all costs. "Yes, I remember the restaurant. I remember everything, Emma. You used to order the club sandwich with homemade chips and two extra sides of ranch dressing."

I laughed. "Yes, I had to have my ranch. I'll never forget stealing the pickles off your plate when you weren't looking." Every time he'd turned his head, I'd steal his pickles. I always got away with it, even though I had the sinking suspicion he let me do it on purpose.

Preston finally looked at me. "I knew what you were doing every time."

"Then why did you let me take them?"

His gaze shifted to my lips before looking away. "I figured you were hungry."

I'd wanted him to say it was because he had feelings for me, but of course, that wasn't going to happen. I had a lot of work to do before he'd fess up.

"Emma," a voice called out. Turning my head, I watched John head toward our table, coffee in hand. His wide grin made me smile.

"Hey, John. It's good to see you." I nodded toward the empty table beside us. "Pull up a chair."

With a stony expression, Preston stared at him and it took all I had not to giggle. Was that jealousy peeking through?

John held out his hand to Preston. "You must be Mr. Hale. I'm John Tallman."

Preston looked down at his hand and eventually shook it. "And who are you exactly?"

I cleared my throat, grabbing his attention. "John's the lead singer and guitarist for First Sanity. We watched their audition last week."

"Oh, right," he said, sizing John up. "I vaguely remember."

I tapped John's arm. "You know, Preston used to be in a band. I'm sure he could give you some advice if you needed."

John's eyes lit up. "That'd be great. I'm always looking to

better myself and my crew."

Preston huffed and sat back in his chair, but deep down, I could tell he wasn't really annoyed; he only pretended to be. He could talk for hours about music and never get bored. Whatever wall he had built was a strong one.

"So what would Mr. Chandler say if I asked Emma to join my band?" John asked him.

I choked on my hot chocolate, spewing it all over the table as I tried to hold it in. John winked at me while Preston's jaw clenched. "Sorry," I coughed. "I don't think that's going to happen. I haven't performed in a long time."

"Well then, it might be time to start. Use it before you lose it, and all that jazz. The guys and I think it's a good idea."

I gasped. "You talked to them about it?"

He chuckled. "Yep. They're on board with bringing in a female."

Preston cleared his throat. "Actually, that'll be hard to do, considering we're heading back home in a couple of weeks. You could always hold an audition. That's how I found one of my singers. She had the sexiest voice."

I remembered that day as if it was yesterday. Preston was my friend, and I auditioned just to be funny. I'd always loved to sing, but when I got on stage with him, it was as if I was in a different world. I never wanted to leave.

Heart racing, I slid out of my chair. "Excuse me for a minute. I need to get some napkins."

Preston watched me walk away and everything inside

of me tightened. He used to always say my voice was sexy, however, he never liked hearing other men say it. I walked up to the counter and grabbed a handful of napkins. Turning around quickly, I ran right into a man whose cup dropped to the floor. Luckily, it was empty. "Oh my God, I'm so sorry."

He picked up his cup and chuckled, his bright green eyes staring right into mine. "It's okay. I'm just glad I didn't spill coffee on that pretty dress of yours."

"Me too. It would've been a bitch to wash out."

His gaze roamed over my face and he smiled. "Well, I hope you have a good day. Maybe we'll run into each other again, only without coffee in our hands."

Tossing his cup in the trash can, he walked toward the back of the restaurant and out the other door. "Emma, you ready to go?" Preston asked, his voice right behind me.

I turned around. "Yep." That was when I noticed our empty table. I looked toward the door and saw John flashing a nervous smile at me before walking out. "Where's he going?"

"He had to leave." Preston's lips turned up slightly. "We need to go too, if you don't want to be late."

16

EMMA

Reaching the house after a long day of auditions, I took off my sandals and tossed them at the front door. "Want to take a walk on the beach?"

He stuffed his hands into the pockets of his jeans. "Not really. But I have a feeling you're going to make me."

I shook my head. "No. I can always go by myself." I started toward the back of the house and I could hear him huff.

"Do you enjoy testing my patience?" he asked, catching up to me.

"Do you enjoy testing mine?" I countered. "You should be thankful I can put up with your attitude."

"Not many can."

The dry sand was warm between my toes. "That used to not be a problem before."

He scoffed. "Things change. Most women are afraid of me

now."

"Maybe it's that dark, brooding look you constantly have on your face. It's like you want to kill someone." His attention shot to me and I realized a little too late what I said. I laughed it off. "You need to lighten up and smile once in a while. No self-respecting woman wants to date a gloomy sourpuss."

We walked down the beach in the direction of his parents' house. I wanted to gauge his reaction when we got close to it. I had yet to figure out which one it was. That was, until I saw him stare at the pretty yellow one just a few houses away. It didn't look like the type of house he'd live in, but then again, the circumstances had changed him dramatically. He wasn't always the hardcore killer he was now.

What made my heart hurt was the fact his sister was found dead not far from where we were walking. Eyes burning, I stopped and picked up a seashell, hoping to get my mind off the tragedy. I couldn't imagine the turmoil he was going through by being on the same beach.

"What about you?" he asked.

Clutching the seashell in my hand, I glanced up at him. "What about me?"

He looked down at the shell in my hands. "Are you seeing someone back home? I figured by now you'd be married and have kids."

I scoffed. "Not exactly. I haven't met anyone worth the title of husband. Besides, I've been too busy trying to find my place in the world."

"And you plan on doing that working for Chandler?"

"I do. He's offered me more than anyone else could. I've actually enjoyed working for him. But soon, I'll be handed over to Wade. He's definitely a different man than Glenn." His eyes blazed and I turned away, my body trembling under his stare.

"Have you slept with him?" he asked, almost growling the words.

Sighing, I started walking down the beach. "I don't think that's any of your business."

"It is, more than you know. Now tell me."

I kept walking, but then his hand wrapped around my arm, his grip tight as he turned me around. My breath hitched and I froze. It was the first time he'd really touched me. My breasts pressed against his chest as I tried to breathe.

"I need to know," he murmured, his voice dark. His breaths came out fast, his gaze on my lips.

I threw my arms around his neck and pulled him down into a soul searing kiss, pressing my lips achingly hard against his. He opened up to me almost instantly, pushing his way in. He groaned into my mouth, his arms holding me so tight I could barely breathe. Breaking the kiss first, Preston stepped back, his eyes wild and feral.

"The answer's no," I whispered. "I haven't slept with Wade, or anyone else, for a really long time."

For a second, I thought he was going to take me there right on the beach, but instead muttered to himself, "Fuck me." Then he shook his head. "We can't do this. If you're smart, you'll stay the hell away from me."

I wasn't going to let him push me away. He wanted me. All I had to do was show him he was worthy of love. "I guess it's a good thing I can think for myself." Tonight was too soon, but I was determined to break him down. Blowing out a heavy breath, I nodded toward Glenn's house. "After you."

PRESTON

wanted her. Holy fucking shit, I wanted her so goddamn bad I could taste it. I was so close to fucking her right there on the beach, just throwing her down on the sand so she could feel how much I needed her. By the look in her eyes, she wanted it too. It took all I had to walk away from her.

For the rest of the night, I was tempted to go to her room. Instead, I handled my own business—coming so hard I probably burst a blood vessel—then logged onto my computer to look at the *list*. But every time I got geared up to go for a kill, I stopped at the door, my guns strapped at the hip.

I couldn't leave Emma, not when I'd almost lost her before. Being near my parents' home was a constant mindfuck. There were too many factors closing in on me, especially with Shelly's death. I had to find the sick bastard who killed her.

The sun was already up and I had yet to hear Emma's steps

on the hardwood floors above. Mrs. Walker was in the kitchen making breakfast when I walked in. She looked over at me and smiled. After my mother and sister were killed, Glenn had hired her to cook for me and my dad. I don't think I ever thanked her for that.

"Good morning," she greeted, her voice soft. "You hungry?" She handed me a plate with a large biscuit and sausage gravy poured over top of it.

"I guess I am," I said, taking the plate. Grabbing a bottle of water out of the refrigerator, I sat at the table to eat my food. "How long are you going to be here this morning?"

She glanced at the clock on the wall. "Hmm . . . probably another couple of hours. Why do you ask?"

I finished the biscuit and rinsed the plate off in the sink before putting it in the dishwasher. "I need to run out for a few minutes. I wanted to make sure Emma wasn't alone."

She waved me off. "Go. She'll be fine. I won't let anyone come in here."

I didn't want to leave, but I had to go back to my house. There was something there I was missing; I had to find it. Since it was early morning, the beach was vacant. I made the walk in short time.

Everything was quiet when I entered my house. Cameron's room was still in disarray, but I wasn't ready to move anything yet. I kept thinking a clue was going to jump out at me, yet there was nothing. As far as I could tell, not a single thing had been taken. Glenn had had his friend at the police department dust for prints, but they couldn't find anything.

My phone rang and I wasn't surprised to see Glenn's name pop up on the screen. "What's going on?" I answered.

"Just checking up on you, son. I wanted you to know I visited your father before I left yesterday."

Clenching my teeth, I fought back the guilt. "And?"

"His depression's gotten worse. He really wants to see you."

"Not until I figure everything out," I snapped.

"What if you don't? Are you just going to let him die without seeing you again? You're all he has left."

"And I have nothing," I countered. "I've given up everything to do what I do. I don't have a family like you, or a billion-dollar company. I'm alone on this God-forsaken earth."

"No, you're not. You have me, and it appears you have Emma as well."

Closing my eyes, I squeezed my phone, visions of Emma running rampant through my mind. "She doesn't want the real me," I said, hanging up the phone. If she knew what I did for a living, she'd run as far and as fast as she could.

I took one last look at Cameron's room before going downstairs. My mother loved taking pictures and it showed by the family portraits she had hanging on the walls. The last one we ever took was when I was fifteen. My mother and father sat in front of me and Cameron; her smiling happily, while I tried to stay cool.

Cameron had kept poking me in the side, trying her best to make me laugh. It just so happened, the photographer got me as I smiled. It was my mother's favorite picture. Cameron looked just like her, with her bright, blonde hair and wide eyes. I was more like my father, dark hair and gray eyes.

I had no clue what he looked like now. Was his hair turning gray? Had he lost weight? The guilt plagued me every day. Killing kept my mind off him and every other fucking thing that'd gone wrong in my life. I wanted to numb the pain, but there was a part of me that couldn't let go.

Taking a deep breath, I called Green Meadows to check on my father. I didn't do it often because I hated being reminded of the shitty state he was in.

"Good morning, this is Lexi, how can I help you?"

I paused before responding. "Hey, Lexi. I'm Preston Hale. I'm calling to check up on my father, David Hale. Is there any way I can speak to his nurse?" Her name was Rachel Sparks, a middle-aged divorcee with two kids.

"Sure, hold on while I transfer you."

The line beeped and it rang again. "Hello, this is Rachel," she answered, her voice low and nasally, as if she'd been crying.

"Rachel, it's Preston Hale. I'm calling to check on my dad." She was never one to sugarcoat anything.

She cleared her throat and sniffled. "I was just about to call you."

The only time she ever called was when something was wrong. I was the main point of contact if anything were to happen. My throat tightened and I gripped the phone. "What's wrong?"

"Your father had a stroke this morning. The ambulance just took him to the hospital." She sniffled again. "I don't know what happened. One minute, he was fine, and the next, he started having problems speaking."

As much as I tried to fight it, I couldn't. My eyes burned and I could feel my heart pounding against my sternum. All I wanted to do was rip the fucker out so I wouldn't have to feel. "Will he be okay?" I demanded.

"I don't know," she mentioned sadly. "You might want to go visit him. He asks for you every day."

I couldn't hear anymore. Instead of answering her, I hung up. Hands shaking, I tried to clench them tight, but they still shook. Why did all the fucked up shit have to happen to my family? Everyone in my life got the shitty end of the stick.

Anger boiled in my veins, and for the first time in days, I let it out. I chucked my phone against the wall, loving the sound of it crashing to the floor. I wanted to hit something so hard it'd make my knuckles bleed. I needed the pain, something I could control. Rearing back, I slammed my fist into the wall, the pain shooting up my arm. I did it again and again, growling as the pain grew more intense . . . only there was no blood. It all rushed to my head, my pulse thumping in my ears. Leaning against the wall, I slid down to the floor. How the hell did I get so fucked up?

I closed my eyes, only for them to shoot right back open

as the sound of footsteps vibrated on the back deck. Funneling my rage into my trigger finger, I slid my gun out of its holster and held it in my grasp. Whoever it was didn't belong at my house.

EMMA

Mrs. Walker was persistent on me staying put at the house, but I had to find Preston. I knew where he was. To keep her from alerting him, I ate my breakfast and said I was going to hang out in my room and draw. The drop from the balcony wasn't too high, but I copied what Preston had done the other night, and climbed down the wall. Luckily, the windows weren't anywhere near the kitchen.

As fast as I could, I took off down the walkway to the beach. Other than a man letting his chocolate Lab play in the ocean, there wasn't anyone else around. I didn't know what I was going to do when I saw Preston, but I knew it was time to say something. He wasn't going to let me in without telling him the truth.

I took the stairs one at a time up to the back porch, until a loud thump came from inside and then another, followed by

Preston's shouts of anger. My feet moved of their own accord and I raced to the door, not even caring what kind of danger I might be in. When I got to the back door, I carefully pried it open, only to stop dead in my tracks. Preston's eyes were wild as he pointed his gun right at my head.

"Oh my God," I gasped, backing into the wall with my hands up. For a split second, I actually feared for my life. Sneaking up on a trained killer hadn't been the smartest move.

Preston's eyes widened in terror and he quickly lowered the gun to the coffee table. "What the fuck were you thinking, Emma? I could've killed you!" he shouted.

My breaths came out in rapid pants. I had to wait for the lightheadedness to subside before I could talk. "I'm sorry. I realize that now."

He ran his hands angrily through his hair, his chest heaving up and down. "Holy fuck," he growled, pacing the room. "Goddammit. How did you find me? You're supposed to be at the house."

I lowered my hands and approached him slowly. "Glenn told me this was where you grew up," I mentioned cautiously.

His whole body tensed and he froze. I could tell he'd barely slept by the look in his tired eyes. They were red, as if he'd held back tears. My heart broke for him, for his losses. The kind of pain he went through every day had to be unimaginable.

"Why would he tell you that?" he demanded.

I moved closer, circling around the couch. "I know a lot of things, Preston." My gaze shifted to the gun on the table and then back to him. I had to get to him before he ran away. "I know about your mother and sister. And even about your father."

He sucked in a breath and stared at me, the pain in his gray eyes making my chest ache.

I fought back the tears as I closed the distance. There were three holes in the wall just behind him, no doubt from his own fists. I was so close to reaching out to him, but he stepped away, the pain on his face turning to rage.

"He had no fucking right to tell you. It's none of your business." Phone in hand, he stormed to the door.

"I know what you are!" I shouted.

He stopped at the door, back rigid.

I waited for him to turn around, but he didn't. "The night I was taken, I saw something. I didn't understand what was going on, and it terrified the shit out of me." Again, he didn't turn around, so I moved even closer, almost closing the distance. "I followed you to Myrtle Beach, Preston."

He jerked around, his expression torn. "What did you see?" His gaze penetrated right through me.

Reaching down, I grabbed one of his hands that was clutched into a tight fist and held it between my hands. I brought it up to my heart and held it tight while looking into his eyes. "I saw you kill someone," I whispered. He looked as if he was going to pull away, but I held on tighter. "You're not going to walk away from me. I won't let you . . . not this time."

"So you're not afraid of me?" he asked, his voice guarded.

I shook my head. "Never. I've always felt safe with you."

"Even knowing what I am? That I kill people?"

"I do," I replied with a nod.

He took a deep breath and exhaled slowly. Flattening his fist out, his palm stretched out over my heart. I could see him opening up, and I didn't want to divulge the next bit, but I had to get everything in the open.

"Glenn told me everything that night."

His jaw stiffened. "That night? What the fuck does that mean?"

Releasing a heavy sigh, I averted my gaze. He pulled away from me and crossed his arms over his chest, his narrowed gaze staring daggers right through me.

"It was Glenn and his sons who took me that night. After I saw you kill that man, I'd called him and told him I was leaving town. But, as it turns out, he'd had you followed, so he already knew I was there. That's when he, Ian, and Bryce broke into the house and took me before I could leave."

"Motherfucker," he growled.

I looked sheepishly down at the floor. "That's not all," I confessed. "There's something else I need to tell you." By the wild look in his eyes, he was on the edge, but I couldn't stop now. "I know I probably shouldn't, but I want you to find out from me first. That way you know I'm here because I *want* to be, not because someone willed it so."

When I looked up at him, realization dawned on his face. He was a smart man and had put the pieces together. "Fuck me," he snapped. "Chandler hired you to get to me, didn't he?"

Sadly, I nodded. "I wasn't aware of it until he took me that night. He thought I could help you. Apparently, he knew we were close in college."

"This is bullshit." He turned to walk out the door, but I grabbed his arm. I refused to let go.

"No, it's not. You need help, Preston. But this killing worthless piece of shits who rape and hurt innocent people? That's your job; it's what you do. The world is a better place without them. I get that, and support you in every aspect. *However*, shutting yourself off from the people who care about you is a different story."

He spun around. "So he took it upon himself to tell you my life story, huh? All of it?"

I swallowed hard and nodded. "He also told me why you left without a trace, that it was you who saved Janie from being raped. Apparently, she wasn't the first of his victims."

His eyes blazed. "To this day, I can still hear her screams."

I remembered talking to her a few days after it happened. She ended up transferring to a different school. "She was terrified," I murmured, "but she wanted desperately to find the person who saved her, so she could thank them. If I could do what you do, I would do it in a heartbeat."

He scoffed. "I fucking kill people, Emma. And what's even more fucked up is that I love it. I *need* it. I don't want to just kill those bastards, I want to torture them, to make them pay for what they've done. I want—"

"To find the man who killed your mother and sister," I finished for him. "You love to kill the bad guys because it helps sustain the guilt you feel. You can't save your family, but you can save others."

Closing his eyes, he released a shaky breath. "Nothing I do will bring them back."

I moved closer, my body so close to his. "No, but it's not too late for you. The Preston I fell in love with years ago is still inside you."

Shaking his head, he averted his gaze. "He doesn't exist anymore."

I touched his cheek, gently turning him to face me. "Yes, he does. You are him, you just have to stop pushing me away." My heart thundered in my chest and I could hear it beating in my ears. I didn't want to waste another second. And so, for the second time in two days, I found myself wrapping my arms around his neck, and pressing my lips to his.

It was as if everything fired to life. I remembered what it was like to be near him, to see his smiling face when we'd talk about music. The old Preston was still there; I could feel him in the way he touched me.

He gripped me around the waist and held me to him, his mouth desperately seeking mine as I wrapped my legs around his hips. His groans made me tremble and I lost myself in his touch. Leaning me against the wall, he lifted my bra and cupped my breast in his hand. Shifting me up, he took my nipple between his teeth and flicked it with his tongue.

Closing my eyes, I moaned and held his head against me, my insides tightening. I could feel the blood rushing to the spot between my legs, making me ache to feel him inside of me. Only one gentle stroke and I would be completely lost and at his mercy.

"Preston," I breathed, arching my back. I kept waiting for him to push me away, but he didn't. His kisses only grew more urgent as his arousal rubbed against my core.

Reaching behind my back, he unclasped my bra, letting it fall to the floor. He stood back and looked up and down my body, his cock getting harder between my legs. "You are so fucking beautiful," he murmured, sliding a strand of hair off my forehead. "I shouldn't want this. I don't want to hurt you."

"I know you won't," I answered him softly. "I'll be okay."

Slowly, he leaned forward and placed his forehead to mine, breathing me in. He was a dangerous man, yet so gentle with his touches. His hands were used to kill people, but with me they caressed and smoothed away my fears. Would it last? I sure hoped so.

My God, I'm falling for him. Just like I had all those years ago, right before he left without a trace. My only fear now was that he'd leave again and never look back.

Carrying me up the stairs, I couldn't even see anything other than his face, his eyes staring into mine as he kissed me. "If it gets to be too much, just tell me to stop," he whispered, his voice raw with need.

I nodded, understanding his concern, but I really wanted

it to happen. "I need you to take this off," I demanded, tugging at his shirt.

He smirked and lifted one arm. I promptly pulled his shirt over his head and he let it fall to the floor. I ran my hands over his bare arms and inspected his body as he opened a door and carried me inside. Pulling back his comforter, he let it crumple on the ground. "It's full of dust," he explained, as he gently laid me down on his king-size bed.

Starting at my lips, he trailed his finger the length my neck, in between my breasts, and down to my shorts. Sliding them down my legs, he tossed them to the side. His hands were warm as he ran them up my legs, spreading them wide. I watched him slink along like a tiger, all sleek muscle and predatory eyes, as he took me in, laying completely open to him.

Sliding off the bed, he walked over to his balcony door and opened it wide, letting the wind blow the sheer, gray gossamer curtains around inside his room. The sun glittered across the ocean water as the waves crashed against the shore.

It was all so perfect.

Preston lowered his shorts to the floor and slowly climbed back on the bed. He rested off to my side, his thick length pressing into my thigh as he turned me to him. "Most people don't know the real me, Emma. I don't even think I know who I am anymore."

"That's why I'm going to help you," I murmured wholeheartedly. "We can do this together."

Leaning down to place a kiss on my pert nipple, he lifted himself over me, spreading my legs with his knee. Once he'd covered my body with his, he leaned on his elbows to keep his full weight off me. There was uncertainty on his face and I wished I could take away those feelings, but it was going to take time. All I knew was, I wanted him to take me, to claim me for his own—leave his mark on me.

"I love the way you look at me," he claimed, brushing his fingers down my cheek. "I've never had anyone see me the way you do. That's why I always kept my distance, even back in college; I didn't want to hurt you."

"I'm a big girl," I said, kissing his fingers as he brushed them over my lips. "I think I've proved that by now."

He looked deeply into my eyes. "So you have."

"And if we cross this line, things will have to be different between us," I admitted tenderly. "Is that a risk you're willing to take?"

He lowered his lips to mine and I closed my eyes, loving the way my lips tingled every time they touched his. "Yes," he answered. "I'd risk just about anything for you."

Looking at him, I smiled and wrapped my legs around his waist, feeling his cock jump in anticipation as I rubbed against it. "Then let's do this."

Ever so gently, Preston unhooked my legs and crawled down my body. Lowering his head, he flicked his tongue across my clit. I gasped.

When he chuckled, his breath fanned across my body,

making it even more sensitive. I'd only had one guy go down on me in my lifetime and it actually sucked. But Preston . . . his tongue worked wonders. Every time he pushed his tongue inside of me, he rolled it around, tasting me while nuzzling my clit with his nose, keeping me stimulated.

"Preston," I moaned, fisting my hands in his hair. I was so close.

He hummed over my center, making me convulse. "Let me make you come."

It brought me to the brink once I saw how aroused he was, his hips thrusting against the bed in sync with the flicks of his tongue. I screamed out his name as the force of my release had me arching off the bed, my hands holding him still as I grinded against his face.

Slowly, I released my hands and brought them to my chest, where my heart thumped wildly. That was the best orgasm I'd had in years.

"I think you're ready now." He smiled as he wiped his mouth on the back of his arm.

Leaning over me, he rocked his hips against mine, using his thumb to push his arousal along my slit, getting it nice and wet. Then, the tip found its mark, pushing inside, stretching me. Taking a deep breath, I closed my eyes as he pushed in the rest of the way. The pain of it made my eyes water, but it was a good pain. In fact, I needed more.

"You can go harder. I promise I won't break."

"Are you sure?" he asked.

Capturing his face in my hands, I bit his lip and sucked on it as hard as I could. He growled low and gripped the edges of the pillow beneath my head. I loved that he was worried about me, and it made me care about him more than ever. But what I *really* needed to feel was the heat I knew he restrained deep inside of him.

"Yes, now stop holding back."

Almost immediately, his breathing picked up and his eyes darkened, the intensity building in the room. I shivered in response and gripped my legs tighter around his waist, rocking my hips hard against his. That was his undoing.

Fisting his hands in my hair, he pulled my head to the side and bit down on my neck, his thrusts growing deeper and faster. I screamed out in pleasure, but Preston silenced me by closing his lips over mine. The harder he pushed his body into me, the closer I was to losing control. I could tell he was close. As soon as I started to clench down on him, he released my hair and brought his hands down to my face, keeping his eyes locked on mine.

Digging my nails into his skin, I rode wave after wave of pure bliss, as the longest damn orgasm of my life rocked through my body. It only intensified when Preston growled in my ear, biting down on my lobe as he too released, pulsating inside of me.

Breathing hard, he lifted up on his elbows and stared down at me. I could almost see the old Preston looking back at me. I smiled. Things were about to change.

I didn't realize I'd fallen asleep until I woke up in Preston's bed, two hours later. My pulse spiked when I realized what time it was; we were supposed to listen to more auditions. Preston was nowhere to be found, and his clothes were gone. There was no sound in the house and my first thought was that he left me there.

Gut clenching, I jumped out of bed and hastily put on my clothes, stopping when I noticed one of the pictures on the wall. It was a picture of Preston with his family. His mother and sister were both beautiful. I couldn't believe someone would murder them in cold blood. But then again, we lived in a world with horrible people.

The bedroom door was open, but the other two rooms across the hall were closed up. A sound came from downstairs and I breathed a sigh of relief. At least he hadn't left me there. Creeping down the steps, I peeked around the corner into the living room. Preston's back was to me, but he stood there, staring at the now patched up wall. Before, there had been three large holes.

"Hey," I murmured.

He glanced at me over his shoulder. "Hey." My insecurities must've shown through because his brows furrowed. "You okay?" I nodded and plastered on a smile, but he could see right through it. "You thought I left, didn't you?"

I shrugged. "You do have a habit of walking away from

me."

A sad expression passed across his face. "I'm not going anywhere, Emma. I told you I'd protect you."

"Remember it was Glenn who took me? I'm not in danger."

"Still," he replied. "I'm not letting you go anywhere without me."

"Speaking of going somewhere," I pointed at the grandfather clock in his living room, "we were supposed to be at the theater thirty minutes ago."

He shook his head. "No, we have the day to ourselves. I called and postponed it. We'll listen to the rest of the bands tomorrow. Besides," he said, his voice low, "I didn't want you asking me to take you to that café you like to go to."

That took me aback. "Why not? They have *the* best blueberry scones and hot chocolate."

Crossing my arms, I walked over and leaned against the side of the couch. There was a pan of sheetrock mud on the floor, leftover from when he'd patched up the wall.

He looked over at me, his mouth set in a firm line. "I don't want to have to tell your friend to fuck off again."

"Who?" I shrieked.

"It's pretty obvious, Emma."

Eyes wide, I gasped. "John?"

"Yep."

"Wow, I had no idea."

He stared at me in disbelief. "Really? The first moment I saw him look at you, I knew he was hard up."

I couldn't help but smile. "Jealous?"

He huffed. "I'm not gonna lie, okay? I didn't like him looking at you."

Seeing him actually show another emotion made me smile. "You have nothing to worry about. I know what I want."

"Good. Because I told him you were dating an MMA fighter who would fuck him up if he tried to get in your pants."

I groaned. "Great. Now that's going to make things awkward when I talk to him again. He's one of my top five picks."

"He'll get over it. And if his band wins the spot, *I'll* be the one dealing with him."

"Are you really going to work for Chandler Enterprises?"

He released a long, hard sigh. "I don't know. I'm not sure what I'm going to do anymore."

"I don't care what you do, so long as you don't run away again." Putting my arm around his waist, I snuggled up to him, my gaze fixed on the patched wall. "By the way, why did you do that?"

He paused, staring at the wall. "Many reasons. The first being, someone broke into the house and destroyed my sister's room. We dusted for prints and came up empty. I think they were looking for something."

"Glenn had told me about the break in," I said, sliding over so I could look at him. "Do you know who it was?"

The muscles in his jaw ticked. "No. But I think the person who killed my family knew my sister. They had to have used a key to get in. Whatever they were looking for, I don't know if they got it."

"Do you have any idea what it could've been?"

"I don't know at this point," he said with a shrug. "As a kid, I used to try to find Cameron's diary so I could read it and make fun of her. She hid it in a new spot every day to throw me off."

"Maybe that's it. I'm an expert at hiding things. Do you want me to see if I can find it?"

He glanced over at me and frowned. "I found it a long time ago, Emma. There was nothing out of the ordinary in it."

"Then maybe there was something else?" I suggested.

"Yeah, but what? I'm sure my sister had her secrets, but I can't think of a reason why anyone would go as far as to kill her and my mother."

I squeezed his shoulder and rubbed my fingers soothingly over his skin. "I can help you, Preston. Just let me look through her room and if there's anything hidden, I'll find it." I jumped to my feet, but he grabbed my wrist, his expression dangerously serious. It was easy to see why people would be afraid of him.

"I don't want you involved," he growled. "It's too dangerous. Once we're done with the bands, you're going back to Charlotte."

"And what will you be doing, finding the killer on your own? Glenn told me he thinks the girl who was murdered the other week was killed by the same man who took your family."

There was no denying the rage building in his gray eyes.

He squeezed my wrist and pulled me to him. "You're not helping me. That's final."

Lifting my chin, I didn't back down from his stare. "I *am* going to help you, whether you like it or not. I'm not leaving you." I caressed his cheek and felt his tension ease, but only slightly. I still had a lot of work to do on him. "Please don't make me go. Believe it or not, Glenn hired me for a reason. He knew I can handle you and all the scary shit that came along with it." He was only a couple inches taller than me, but I still had to stand on my tiptoes to kiss him. "Let me help you."

His lips responded to mine and I moaned. Lifting his hands to my face, he held me tight. "If things get bad, you're heading back to Charlotte. Until then, you can stay. Deal?"

"Deal," I agreed triumphantly. "Now let me see what I can find in your sister's room." I tried to walk away, but he wouldn't let me go.

"Not yet. There's something else that happened," he hedged, looking almost guilty.

The change in demeanor threw me a bit. "What is it?"

"What all do you know about my father?"

I took a deep breath and felt the burn build behind my eyes. I knew all about Preston and his father, about how he hadn't seen him in years, and I told him as much.

He nodded sadly. "I told myself I wouldn't see him until I killed the fucker who took everything away from us."

"What if that never happens?"

"It will happen," he said, his voice low and dark. "It's only a matter of time."

I threw my hands up in the air. "So you're just going to let your dad die without seeing him again?"

He flinched and turned away. "I found out this morning he had a stroke. They took him to the hospital."

"Oh my God, why didn't you say something sooner? Let's go see him. This will be here when we get back." I started toward the door, but when I turned around, he hadn't moved. "What are you doing? Let's go."

He shook his head. "I can't."

Taking a deep breath, I opened the door slowly, glancing at him over my shoulder. "It's funny . . ."

His gaze narrowed. "What is?"

I stared him down. "I didn't take you as the kind of guy to be scared." With those final words, I walked out the door.

19

PRESTON

The woman was going to drive me in-fucking-sane. I knew the second I let her in, it'd be my undoing. I wasn't ready to see my father, not after staying away for so many years. I tried blaming my fucked up life on him, when in all honesty, it was my own fault. It was better to push everyone away and not give a shit, than deal with the disappointment on their faces when I didn't live up to their expectations.

A part of me wanted to go back to that way of life, but Emma was like a drug. I didn't just want her . . . I needed her. Even now, watching her as she stared out the window of my car, all I could think about was throwing her on my bed and forgetting every fucking thing in my life, except how it felt to be near her.

We pulled into the hospital parking lot and parked; only, I wasn't ready to get out of the car.

Emma grabbed my hand and squeezed. "I know you don't want to be here, but you'll regret it for the rest of your life if something happens to your father and you never made an effort to see him again."

She was right, but I didn't know if I was ready. Getting out of the car, it felt like my shoes were full of lead. It took all I had to get inside the door.

The lady at the front desk was busy typing away on her computer, but when we walked up, she stopped and smiled at us. "May I help you?"

"We're here to see David Hale. He was brought in this morning. I'm Preston Hale, his son."

"Of course. Give me one second to see what room he's in," she said, focusing back on the computer. She gave us his room number and directed us to the right set of elevators.

Once we got inside, Emma clasped her hand with mine. "You'll do fine. I promise. I honestly wouldn't know what to do without my dad. I miss my parents so much as it is. I'm proud of you for doing this."

"How often do you see them?" I wondered.

"Usually every weekend when I'm back home. You'll have to come over for Sunday dinner when we get back. My parents would love to see you again." I'd met them a few times back when we were in school. They used to come up and watch us play at the college club. "However, we might have to come up with a story on where you disappeared to," she added. "I talked about you all the time."

"I'm sure we can think of something." For the longest time, I thought she and everyone else would've forgotten about me. Looking back, I'd give anything to have done things differently.

The elevator doors opened and we walked into the hallway and down to my father's room. Emma stopped at the door, placing her hand on the handle. "Ready?"

No.

She opened the door and I walked through. The shades were up and the sun shone into the room. My father was asleep, tubes going in and out of his body.

"Wow," Emma whispered, holding onto my arm. "You look just like him. I saw your pictures, but it's different seeing him in person. Do you have the same color eyes?"

I nodded, not able to take my eyes off him. He was a lot skinnier than the last time I saw him. His hair had more gray, and his once tanned skin was now pale and papery thin. It was hard to believe that the man before me was the same man who used to be a skilled assassin. Everyone had looked up to him and Glenn, including the Chandler brothers.

My dad's eyes fluttered and when they opened, I held my breath. His brows furrowed, and then recognition shown on his face. "Preston? Is that you?" he asked, his voice weak.

Emma squeezed my hand. "I'm going to give you some privacy. I'll be sitting right outside the door."

I couldn't summon the words, so I squeezed her hand back. My father watched her walk out the door and then turned his head to me. I met his gaze. "Feeling okay?"

He coughed. "Been better." Then he nodded toward the door. "She your wife?"

When he talked, only the right side of his mouth worked. The stroke must've hit him hard.

"No," I said, trying to muster a smile. There was a chair beside his bed, so I shuffled over and sat down. "She's a close friend of mine. I met her in college."

He slowly turned his head to face me. "Was she the one in your band? She looks familiar."

"How did you know that?"

He tried to smile again, only the right side of his face working. "I know everything about you, son. Even though you kept your distance from me, I never kept it from you."

I lowered my head, breaking eye contact. How was I supposed to respond to that? "I'm sorry. I should've come sooner. It's just . . . everything's been fucked up."

"I know," he murmured. "Glenn didn't hold back when he told me what you were going through. I just wish I could've been there. I never would've pushed you so hard to be a part of the team if I'd known."

I shook my head, staring at my clasped hands. "I like being part of the team." *I like killing worthless fuckers.* But I didn't want to tell him that. It was wrong to love it so much.

"Look at me, son," my father commanded, his voice weak.

Taking a deep breath, I blew it out slowly and looked at him. He had tears in his eyes and I felt everything inside me break.

"I've missed you. You have no idea how long I've waited to see you. It kills me that you shut me out."

My eyes burned so fucking bad. If I hadn't been sitting, the grief would've brought me to my knees. "I shut everyone out. I felt like you blamed me for mom and Cam's deaths. It was too much, so I blocked everything out. It was easier that way."

He broke down and let his tears fall. The only other time I'd seen him cry was at the funeral. "I never blamed you, Preston. I was angry, but not at you. Losing your mother and sister in the way we did was the absolute worst thing that could ever happen. I was supposed to protect them and I failed. It's not something a husband or a father can bear." Blowing out a shaky breath, he closed his eyes, lips trembling. "I've wanted to tell you this for so long." His words choked up in his throat. "You just never came."

A tear worked its way out and slid down my cheek. I hastily wiped it away. "I wanted to wait," I confessed. "You're not the only one who feels like they failed."

"But you are *not* a failure. Think of all the people's lives you've saved, getting rid of those worthless bastards."

I shook my head. "It's not enough. I didn't want to come to you until I killed the one. The one that haunts us. The one who ripped our family apart."

My father sighed. "It's been thirteen years, Preston. If we haven't caught him now, we might never will. Knowing you're trying to find him is enough for me."

Reaching over, I placed my hand on his shoulder and

squeezed. It was one part of his body I knew he could feel my touch. "I'm so sorry, Dad."

"It's okay," he murmured. "You're here now."

"Now all you have to do is get better."

A sad smile spread across his face. "You know that's not going to happen, son. I'm losing this battle."

I knew it, but I didn't know what to say. The only thing I could do was make sure I killed the man who took our family from us, *before* he passed away. "I should probably go, so you can rest." I stood, but saw the panic build in his eyes.

"No," he pleaded. "Don't go. All I ask is one more night with your old man."

We used to be close, always fishing and camping together every chance we got. "Emma's outside. I don't want to leave her alone."

"You don't have to. She can stay too. Glenn bribed the hospital into allowing me everything I needed. I *need* you here. Please." I gave in with a nod and he breathed a sigh of relief. "Thank you. I want to know everything about you and this girl."

I chuckled. "It's a long story."

He smiled. "We've got all night."

20

EMMA

"Thank you," Preston said, stopping me at the car with his hands on my hips.

I leaned against him and he held me tight. The sun peeked through the trees in the distance, and my eyes felt heavy. "You're welcome," I replied with a yawn. "I enjoyed talking to your dad. It was awesome hearing stories from when you were a boy." Turning around, I gazed up into his tired, gray eyes. "All your fears were for nothing. He loves you so much." But I could see the pain on his face.

"He's not going to last long in there. I have to work fast."

Once we were in the car and on our way, I asked, "Why didn't you tell him someone broke into your house?"

He sighed. "I wanted to, but more stress is the last thing he needs. It'll only make things worse."

Clasping his hand in mine, I held it tight. "How about,

after we finish at the theater, we go back to your house and I search through your sister's room? Doesn't hurt to have another pair of eyes."

We stopped at a stoplight and he looked over at me. "You sure you want to do that?"

I nodded. "Maybe there's something you can't see that I can. Girls are good at hiding things," I said with a wink.

He smiled and blew out a heavy breath. "Okay, we can go tomorrow. Tonight, it's just me and you. There's still so much you don't know."

"And I'm not going anywhere." We were coming up on the café by the theater. "I lied," I said, pointing. "I know we don't have much time, but I need my hot chocolate. If you pull over, I can run in really quick."

"You haven't changed a bit," he said with a laugh. There weren't any parking spaces in front of the café, so he pulled around back.

I got out and shut the door, bending down so I could see him. "Want anything?"

"Coffee, black."

I winked. "Got it. You sure you don't want to go in with me, in case John's in there?"

Preston's mischievous smirk made me shiver. "I don't think I have anything to worry about on that end."

His confidence made me wonder what more he'd said to John than he'd previously let on. Shaking my head, I took off across the street and around both corners of the café to the front door. It was a busy Wednesday morning. People were everywhere, trying to get their morning coffee runs in before the midweek slump.

I ordered our drinks and snuck a bite of my blueberry scone while waiting for the girl to put whipped cream in my hot chocolate. Preston's coffee smelled wonderful, but I hated the taste of it. My phone rang, so I moved down to the end of the counter and set the coffee down to reach for my phone. It was Andrea.

"Hey," I answered.

"Hey, yourself. Been too busy to call me?"

If only she knew. "You have no idea." I laughed. "I have so much to tell you. Unfortunately, I can't say too much at the moment. I'm in a public place."

She gasped. "Did you and Preston have *sex*?"

"Of course, that'd be the first thing you thought of." I paused for a second and smiled. "But yes, we did. Things between us have been going amazing, for the most part. But that doesn't even begin to cover what's been going on."

"Now I'm intrigued. You'll have to tell me all about it. Looks like I'll have plenty of time on my hands here for the next few months."

"Oh yeah, why is that?" The lady at the counter handed me my hot chocolate. I mouthed the words 'thank you' to her, and slipped the small paper bag with my scone inside my purse. Picking up the drinks, I jostled my way to the front door.

She sighed. "The doctor wants me to take it easy.

Apparently, Matthew wants to come out early."

"Oh no. Is Cliff going to stay home and help you?"

"Yes, he'll be here with me for part of the time. My mom's going to help too."

Hands full, I looked at the door. A little girl with pig tails saw my dilemma and hopped out of her seat to open it for me. "Aw, thank you, sweetheart." Once outside, all I had to do was get to the car without spilling our drinks. "Sorry about that," I said to Andrea. "I'm trying to keep myself from spilling fiery hot liquids all over myself."

"I understand." She giggled.

I cringed. "Ugh. I need to check up on my parents. With everything going on, I haven't had time."

"I'm sure they'll understand. You work for a powerful man." She had *no* idea.

The phone was about to slip away from my ear so I stopped and set the drinks on one of the small tables. "That I do. I promise once I'm done in Charleston, I'll head up to Maine. I'm hoping Preston will decide to come with me."

"Oh my God, that would be amazing," she gushed. "It'll be just like when we were in college."

I doubted that, but I was hoping it'd help him. "All right, babe, I need to get going. We have to listen to a few more bands before we make our final decision."

"It's a shame Silent Break couldn't make a debut again. You guys were amazing."

Memories of us on stage at the local college club and at frat parties flashed through my mind. "Yes, we were, but it might be a little too late for that."

"Never know."

I snorted. "I'll talk to you later. Make sure to get your rest." We said our goodbyes, and I slipped my phone back into my purse. Preston and I only had a couple of minutes left before we had to be at the theater. Picking up the drinks, I started toward the side of the building. Before I could turn the corner, I came to a screeching halt, narrowly missing a man rounding the same corner.

I sucked in a breath and closed my eyes, heart racing. The man laughed. "We seriously need to stop meeting like this."

My eyes flew open at the recognition of his voice. It was the man I'd bumped into at the café the other day. "Yes, we do. It would've been bad today," I said, nodding toward the cups in my hands.

He chuckled. "Yes, it would. Did you just move here? I've never seen you at the café until just recently."

"No, I'm here on business. I'll be going home soon." I really needed to get back to the car, but I didn't want to be rude.

Stepping to the side, he waved me by. "I don't want to keep you. Maybe I'll see you again."

I smiled to be polite. "Maybe." I walked past him and around the last corner.

Preston waited outside the car, leaning against the door. When he saw me, his shoulders relaxed. "Everything okay?" he called out.

I hurried across the street and handed him his coffee. "Yeah. Andrea called and then I ran into someone."

His eyes darkened. "John?"

"No," I said with a laugh. "I bumped into him the other day, and I almost spilled our drinks on him this time. I swear, I'm the clumsiest person in that café."

Preston winked. "What else is new?"

Rolling my eyes, I smacked his arm. "Let's go. We have a busy day. I'm ready to get it started."

"Have you decided which bands you liked?" I looked over at Preston, the golden rays of the sun setting brought out a sparkle in his tired eyes. We were on my balcony, with notes from the auditions scattered in front of us on the table. The day had been long and we were kicking up our feet for the rest of the night.

He handed me his notes with his two band choices on it. "These guys were good."

I rocked back and forth in my rocking chair, hating the fact I had to pick only five bands out of the amazing group of people we had the honor to audition.

I passed him my choices. "So are these."

His lips pursed when he read the last band name on my list, First Sanity. He knew it was John's group. "How did I know?"

I snatched the paper out of his hand. "They are really

talented, and he has the personality for this type of work. He'd be good with the crowd. Besides, you're the one who'll be guiding him. That's your job. I'll be working as Wade's assistant before too long."

He huffed. "I don't think that's going to work. I don't want you traveling everywhere with him."

I shrugged and tucked our notes back into my notebook, before the pages could fly away with the wind. "It's my job."

Getting to his feet, he reached for my hands, lifting me up. He tilted my chin and brushed the hair out of my face, holding it back with his hands. "You could always work for me. Wade can find someone else. I'm sure Glenn wouldn't mind."

I wrapped my arms around his waist. "If I worked for you, we'd never get anything done."

"We've done just fine here," he said in all seriousness.

Leaning into his touch, I smiled. "You know, I never told you what Andrea said."

His brows furrowed. "About what?"

"She thinks we need to bring Silent Break back to life. With Glenn backing us up, we could really do something with ourselves. I'm sure Cliff would love to be a part of it."

A heavy sigh escaped his lips. "We've been out of it for so long, Emma. I wouldn't know where to begin."

Bringing my hands to his cheeks, I leaned up and kissed him. "That's what you have me for. I was always the smartest in the group."

Preston's eyes darkened, his smile fading. His body

grew hard against my stomach and I bit my lip. "If you were the smartest, you wouldn't be here with me right now," he murmured.

I shrugged. "Maybe, but I kind of like having you around. In fact," I said, reaching between his legs. His cock jumped when my hand slid down his shorts, earning a strangled groan. "There's something I need from you right now."

He lowered his forehead to mine, his breathing deep as I massaged him. "Fuck, you're killing me. I'd do anything to have you in bed every single, fucking night."

Lifting up, I sucked his lip between my teeth. "What's stopping you?"

"Not a damn thing." His hands snaked up my T-shirt and he tore it away from my body, unsnapping my bra next.

The blowing wind sent goose bumps up and down my arms, nipples pebbling. He bent down and closed his lips over a hardened peak and sucked, pulling and biting until I cried out in pleasure.

Sliding his lips up my neck, he closed them over my lips. "I used to think about doing this every time I was around you," he murmured low.

I grabbed his hand and slid it under the waistband of my jeans. Using my hand to push his fingers against my wet heat, I moaned. "And every time I touched myself, I used to imagine it was you."

He paused and stared down at me, his eyes wild. Pulling his hand out, he unbuttoned my jeans. As soon as he was done, we worked together to push them down enough to where I could kick them off. Standing before him, naked on the porch, I watched as he tore off his shirt and slid his pants down, never breaking eye contact.

His cock bulged behind his boxers and I bit my lip as he rubbed his thick length through the material, allowing his eyes to travel up and down my body. He then slid his boxers down and stroked himself in long, slow movements. Watching me watch him was the single most erotic thing I'd ever seen.

"Come here," he demanded, his gray eyes blazing with an intensity that made me tremble.

I'd never seen anyone stare at me like that. It was kind of scary, but good, in a primal way.

Stepping toward him, my excitement was at an all-time high. What pleasure would he wring from me this time?

Preston wasted little time, he grabbed my arm and flipped me around. "Grab the chair," he grunted.

I bent over to put my hands on the arms of the porch chair, just as I felt him press against me, his knee nudging my legs apart. Grabbing onto my ass, he pulled me wide, running his tongue over my center, tongue lapping at my clit. Before I could groan in appreciation, he stood, tip pushing against my entrance.

Growling deep in his chest, he plunged in as far as he could go. I screamed and dug my nails into the chair as he bounced me up and down his cock, hard. My core stretched to fit all of him, but the pain of it made my eyes water.

Preston leaned over me and bit down on the soft spot behind my ear, sending chills cascading down my body. What made it even better was that he didn't stop there. Reaching around me, he fused both of his hands to my breasts, squeezing my nipples.

An orgasm built between my legs and judging by his strangled groan, he knew I was about to come. Standing up, he pulled me off his dick long enough to sit on the chair and pull me up on his lap.

"I want to see you when you come. Ride me," he commanded, squeezing my ass.

Lifting my hips, I sat down on him until I got a good rhythm—my clit rubbing against him in the most delicious way. My body clenched. I was so close. "I'm going to come," I warned.

"Keep going, baby. I'm gonna come inside you."

I threw my head back as my insides tightened. Just the thought of him releasing inside me sent me over the edge. "*Yes*," I cried breathlessly. My movements slowed as my climax hit, stomach quivering uncontrollably.

His fingers dug into my hips and he held me down on his cock as he took over, pushing up into me at a furious pace. I braced my arms on the back of the chair as he chased his own release. Then he yelled out, all hot and primal, his body jerking in spasms.

Laying my head on his shoulder, my heart beat out of control. "Now *that's* what I'm talking about," I marveled.

Brushing my hair to the side, he gently kissed my neck and held me tighter. "Just remember, angel. You asked for it. Every night, I'm going to find you and take you. There's no turning back."

Moaning, I pulled my head back enough to come face to face. Nipping his bottom lip between my teeth, I said, "I'm counting on it."

Later that night, we laid in bed and listened to the crashing waves just outside, the wind blowing the salty sea air into the bedroom. Preston traced his fingers along my side in the same pattern, over and over.

"What are you drawing?"

His fingers stopped. "Sorry. I didn't realize what I was doing."

"It's okay," I said, turning around to face him. "I was trying to figure out what it was." I snuggled up closer to him while he looked down at me, leaning on his elbow. There was something in his eyes he was trying to hold back, like a caged animal ready to be set free.

"I was tracing the symbol for my group. Glenn calls us the Circle of Justice." Sitting up, he turned around so his back was to me. He had tattoos across his shoulders, arms and back; there were so many. "If you look just below my neck, you'll see the sword and scales. The scales are supposed to represent justice."

There was also a snake wrapped around the sword hilt, with a date on the blade. *10/27.* "What does the snake mean?" I asked softly, tracing my fingers across his skin.

He laid back down and slowly released his breath, his eyes churning with emotion. "It represents me. I strike hard and fast, killing every enemy that crosses me."

"And the date in the blade?"

Swallowing hard, he closed his eyes, his jaw muscles tensing. "It's the day my mother and sister were killed."

I had a feeling that was it, but I needed to make sure. "I'm so sorry," I whispered. "I want you to be able to tell me these things."

He opened his eyes. "If I told you some of the things I've done, you'd run away and never look back."

Letting the sheets fall from my body, I sat up. "That's not true. I've already seen you *kill* a man, Preston. And I'm still here. I'm not afraid of who you are."

He sat up and leaned against the headboard. "You say that now, but what's gonna happen when I get back to my job? Will you be waiting for me when I get home, after I've just ended someone's life?"

I wasn't going to let him scare me. Keeping my gaze on his, I straddled his lap, loving the way his cock twitched between my legs. "If you let me, I'll be there for you every night." I clutched his face in my hands. "You're a hero, Preston. Think of all the innocent lives you've saved over the years. Who knows, I might've been one of them. I used to walk by those woods all the time, right where you saved Janie."

He hung by a thread and I didn't know if it was because he hadn't killed in a few days, or if it was something else. I didn't want to keep him from doing his duty to our country.

"How many people have you killed, Preston?"

For the longest time, he just stared at me, as if contemplating on whether or not he should answer.

"You can tell me."

This time, he averted his gaze. "Three-hundred and eighty-seven."

Frozen, I sat there speechless. That was a lot of people. I'd been thinking more like dozens, not hundreds.

He flit his eyes back to mine. "Ready to run yet?"

His voice snapped me back. "Stop saying that," I huffed. "I'm just a little . . . shocked. That's a lot of people to track down."

"It's what I do, angel."

"Does everyone in your group go after the same kind of people? What about Wade, Ian, and Bryce? What does Glenn have them do?" It was hard to picture them doing the same thing as Preston; they were all so different. None of them struck me as assassins. Maybe that was why they were so good at it.

"Glenn has us all in different categories," he stated. "I choose to go after the rapists and child molesters who were let off easy. Wade used to be as active as me, until about two years ago. Now that he's taking over Chandler Enterprises, Glenn wants him to concentrate on that. So he doesn't get called away for missions that often now. But when he does, he hunts down those who go after government officials. His job takes more time to plan."

"Wow," I blurted, completely taken by surprise. "What about Ian and Bryce?"

"Ian hunts down mob leaders and disposes of them. And Bryce spends most of his time training their youngest brother, Reed, out in Wyoming. He'll be inducted into the group soon."

"How long did you have to train?" I wondered.

Sighing, he clutched my arms, pulling me closer. "A couple of years. It's what I did, day in and day out."

"Do you even manage to have a life?"

He shook his head. "Going after those sick fucks is all I want to do. Soon, I'll have to get back to it."

"I know." I leaned down and brushed my lips against his. "Just promise me you won't shut me out again."

He slid his hands to my face. "I won't, as long as you swear not to run."

We kissed again and his body sprung to life. "Never."

21

EMMA

The door to the gym opened and Preston emerged, his body drenched in sweat. It was nine the next morning and we'd called and given Mrs. Walker the day off.

I looked up from my breakfast and smiled. "I called the bands about the final auditions."

"Oh yeah?" He wiped the sweat off his forehead with a towel. "How'd that go?"

"Good, but I think you scared the shit out of John. He wasn't his usual playful self."

He tried to hide his smile and failed. "I'm glad the boy took my advice."

I rolled my eyes. "I do know how to take care of myself, you know. All I had to do was tell him no."

Grabbing a cup of coffee, he sat down at the table with me, eyes dark. "Some people don't know the meaning of that word."

Sadly, he was right. "I know," I whispered. His overprotectiveness was always going to be there; nothing would change that. It made me wonder if he'd been that way before his mother and sister were murdered.

Sliding the chair back, I stood and stretched. My muscles were sore from the night before, but I was ready to go to his house and search through Cameron's room. "You ready to go to your house? There's a lot of work to do. I don't know when Glenn's going to want me back in Charlotte, so I want to help you as much as I can."

Preston finished his coffee, his lips set in a firm line as he nodded. "Let's go."

The walk was silent, and I knew it was because he hated going there. I couldn't imagine the strength it took to walk into that house each and every time.

Preston opened the door and everything looked the same from where we left it. The holes in the wall were patched up, and ready to be painted. I thought he was going to work on it, but was surprised when he followed me up the stairs to his sister's room.

"You going to help me?" I asked, stopping at Cameron's door.

His jaw clenched as he stared at the door. "I don't know what I'm doing."

Gently, I opened the door and walked inside. Cameron's room was a mess. I glanced back at Preston, my heart aching at the look on his face. I could see the pain. "Why don't you take a seat and tell me about her? Might help for you to talk it out."

His eyes darted my way. "Nothing helps, angel."

"There's nothing wrong with trying." Turning my back, I wanted to give him his space for when he was ready.

There were letters and pictures, all scattered around the floor, many of them of Cameron and her girlfriends . . . but mostly, of her and a good-looking, young man. Only, those pictures were ripped apart. She had a framed picture of him that was broken on the other side of the room. I picked it up, letting the shards of glass fall to the floor.

"Was this her boyfriend?" I asked, facing Preston again. The guy looked familiar but I couldn't place him. I held the picture up and he walked the rest of the way into the room, staring at it.

"His name's Adam Payne. They were together three years before she was killed."

I looked down at the picture. Adam and Cameron looked so happy together, all dressed up for prom. "Where was he that night?" I'd seen it on the news plenty of times, jealous boyfriends killing their girlfriends for one reason or another.

Preston closed the distance. "He was the quarterback at Chapel Hill. The night of the murder, he was playing in the game. Her death fucked him up." He took the picture from my hands. "The day of the funeral, he had to be escorted out; he completely lost it. For a while, everyone thought he'd commit suicide."

"Wow," I gasped. "Have you seen him since then?"

Shaking his head, he set the picture back down on the dresser. "No, but I kept up with him. He went on to finish out his football career at Chapel Hill, and eventually, went on to play pro for Atlanta. He's still there."

Recognition sparked in my mind. *That* was where I knew him from. "No wonder I thought he looked familiar."

He nodded. "He's married now, and one of the best quarterbacks in the NFL. We all thought he'd fuck it up, but he eventually got his shit together."

I scooped more pictures off the floor and put them back in Cameron's dresser. "Sometimes that's hard to do."

Preston grabbed Cameron's senior yearbook off the bed, and sat down on a futon in the corner of the room. He flipped through it, studying every page. "The only person I talked to after that funeral was her best friend, Lainey. I asked her if she knew of anyone who had a key to the house."

"You must've done that recently," I said.

He nodded. "I went to see her right after I figured out what happened here. She didn't know anything."

All the pictures were put back into Cameron's drawers, but I kept out the letters. There were love letters from Adam, and even funny ones from Cameron's friends. I was hoping to find a diary of sorts, but came up empty.

I didn't want to fail. I had to find *something*. Preston's focus was on the yearbook, so I sat beside him and watched him flip through it. He stopped on the page with his sister's senior picture. She had been so beautiful. Now that my hair was grown out, it looked exactly like hers, with golden blonde waves down my back.

"She was really pretty," I whispered.

Preston smiled. "She was. All of my friends had a crush on her. I beat the shit out of one because he tried to spy on her through her bedroom window."

I laughed. "I can see that. You've always been a protective ass."

"Only for those I care about," he murmured, flipping through more pages. Cameron was a popular girl, a cheerleader, and even the homecoming queen. Not only was she beautiful and well-liked, but she was smart as well. The homecoming queen at my high school was never a part of the math team like Cameron had been.

Once he was done looking through the yearbook, he closed it and set it aside.

Taking his hand, I wrapped both of mine around it. "You don't have to answer this if you don't want to, but can you tell me how Cameron was murdered? I have my guesses, but I would like to know the truth."

He closed his eyes and blew out a heavy breath. "Strangled . . . and raped."

"I see," I replied, swallowing hard. That was why he liked to kill rapists. "And there was no DNA on her body, or under her nails? Surely, she fought back."

His eyes flashed open, rage burning inside of them. "She

did, but there was nothing. What really gets me is . . ." Stopping mid-sentence, he jumped to his feet, and paced the room. He ran a hand angrily through his hair and then stopped, keeping his back to me.

I stayed put, my heart beating out of control. "What were you going to say?"

Lowering his head, his shoulders hunched. "She was raped, but not until *after* she was already dead. What gets me though, is that it wasn't forceful. Her body was examined and there was no sign of internal tearing or damage, almost like he did it gently."

"Did he not . . . finish inside her? Couldn't they use that as DNA?"

"No. He was too smart for that. Not sure what he did, but he'd clearly been careful not to leave any traces behind."

I was not expecting to hear that. "Do you think it was another lover?"

He jerked around. "My sister wasn't like that. She never would've cheated on Adam."

I held up my hands. "I'm not saying she did. It just sounds like something an admirer would have done. Not to mention, the pictures of Cameron and Adam are all destroyed or ripped apart. Obviously, it's someone who wanted her."

"It could've been anyone," he huffed. "All the guys at school wanted in her pants, even older men fancied her."

I had no doubt. Looking at her senior class picture, Cameron could've passed for twenty-five. "Did Adam ever have a key to the house?" I wondered.

Preston shrugged. "Don't know. There are lots of questions I should've asked him, but I was just a teenager. If I had known what I knew now, it'd be a different story."

I jumped to my feet. "Then let's ask him. Atlanta's not too far away. We could drive out there tomorrow."

"It's been so long," he said with a shake of his head. "And he's a star now. I doubt we could even get near him."

Closing the distance, I grabbed his arms. "I'm sure he hasn't forgotten. This could be what you need." I wasn't going to back down. If I had to figure out a way to see the NFL starter, I'd do it myself.

Preston could see the determination on my face. "Fine. We'll go first thing in the morning."

I had to believe we were one step closer.

22

PRESTON

didn't know if I was ready to see Adam after all these years.
The problem was, he had no clue his soon-to-be visitor was
me. Through Glenn's connections, Emma and I were able to
get access into the stadium. It'd been a long time, but I had no
doubt he'd recognize me the second he looked at my face.

"What did Glenn say?" Emma asked.

I looked over at the rookies who were still practicing on
the field. "That we were reporters for a sports magazine and
we wanted to run a story on him."

"Great," she groaned. "What if he sees you and freaks out?"

I had an idea. "He won't. He'll see you first. Then, when he
gets closer, I'll make sure he doesn't walk away." After Adam
heard what I had to say, I believed he'd want to help.

Minutes later, Adam emerged onto the field and I turned
my back.

"He's coming," Emma said. We were far enough away in the stands to where no one could hear us on the field. "Good afternoon, Mr. Payne. I'm Emma. It's so nice to finally meet you."

"Likewise," Adam replied. Once I heard them shake hands, I turned around. Adam glanced at me and smiled, but it slowly faded when recognition flashed across his face. "Preston?" His eyes darted to Emma, then back to me. "What are you doing here?"

I held out my hand and he shook it. "I didn't know if you'd want to see me or not. It's been a long time."

He let my hand go. "It has. I guess I've stayed away from Charleston so I wouldn't be reminded . . ."

I nodded. "That's why we staged this meeting. You might not have seen me otherwise."

Eyes narrowed, Adam crossed his arms across his chest. "Then tell me what you're doing here."

Emma stepped back so I could move closer. "Did you hear about Shelly Price? She graduated in my class."

Jaw clenching, he huffed through his nose. "I heard."

"Then I'm sure you know how she was found."

He averted his gaze and nodded, his voice thick. "Just like Cameron."

"Which means, it could be the same guy who killed her."

"How do you know that?" he asked, jerking his head up. "It's been thirteen years."

With a heavy sigh, I knew it hurt him to hear all of this. I could still see the pain on his face after all this time. I couldn't imagine losing Emma the way he lost my sister.

"Someone broke into the house," I confided. "The only room trashed was Cameron's. My guess is they were looking for something. I wanted to see if you might know what it was."

He sucked in a breath, eyes fueled with rage. "Like what?"

I shrugged. "No idea. Maybe a diary or journal of sorts? I found one diary of hers, but there was nothing in it." There had to be another one.

"I know she wrote in one, but she never told me where she kept it," he explained.

We'd just have to look harder when we got back home. "Good. We'll be on the lookout for it. However, I do know they didn't like seeing the pictures of you and Cam. Most of them were destroyed. Do you know of anyone who'd do that?"

Face pale, he shook his head. "No. Have the police found anything?"

I huffed. "There were no fingerprints, but that isn't what bothers me. Whoever it is entered the house with a key. Do you know if Cameron ever gave any out?"

Blowing out a breath, he lowered his head and nodded. "I had one," he confessed. "I used to sneak in all the time when your parents were asleep. But then, I lost the key one day and just started climbing up through her window."

"How did you lose the key?" Emma blurted out.

That was a good question. Adam looked over at her and shrugged. "Don't know. One day it was on my keychain, and the next, it was gone. I never thought too much about it."

Emma met my gaze and my stomach clenched. "Do you think it could be possible?"

I knew exactly what she was implying. Cameron knew her killer. It had been personal. Unfortunately, that meant it was someone close to her . . . and maybe close to Adam.

"What?" Adam asked desperately.

"We think whoever took your key is the one who killed her," I stated. "We just need to figure out who it was."

He threw his arms in the air. "And how are you going to do that? No one's been able to for thirteen years."

"That's because I wasn't ready. Now I'm back."

"What are you, a police officer now?"

I shook my head. "Something much worse than that. I'm sorry for bombarding you with this. Just do me a favor and don't tell anyone I was here asking questions. I'm going to find who took Cameron from us and make the fucker pay."

Adam nodded and shook my hand again, his eyes full of unshed tears.

Once Emma and I got back into my car, I called my dad to check on him. His pneumonia made it hard for him to breathe or talk, so I could only get a few words out of him. It was apparent he was getting worse. Time was running out.

"Do you think we're grasping at straws?" Emma asked. "I mean, what are the chances that Adam's key is the one the killer used to get in?"

I scoffed. "You'd be surprised. You have no idea the kind of shit I've seen. It worries me that the killer might've been a part of her life and we didn't know."

"How are we going to find them?"

"If it's someone from Cameron's past, I'll find them. It'll just take time."

Emma clasped my hand, entwining her fingers with mine. "Not unless we find her diary first."

EMMA

knew before we even sat down to watch the auditions, my first choice would be John's group. And in the end, he smiled at me and waved when Preston told him the good news. I was about to join them when my phone rang. It was Glenn.

"Hey," I answered. I hadn't talk to him since he left.

"Morning. How's everything going?"

"Good. In fact, we just picked a band. They'll be on your doorstep early next week."

"Glad to hear it. Does that mean you and Preston will be coming back as well?" he asked.

I cleared my throat and hurried out of the auditorium for privacy. "Not exactly. I think we might be close to figuring out who killed his family. Plus, his father isn't doing well. Preston isn't going to leave just yet, and I don't want him alone."

He sighed. "I understand. I talked to the hospital yesterday.

David told me Preston came to see him. I'm hoping to get out there again soon. All I can say is thank you for being there for Preston."

"I care about him, Glenn. There's nothing I wouldn't do for him."

"Just be careful. I want you back in one piece. I'm sure you know how dangerous this can get."

"I know." I could hear Preston and John's voices growing closer. "Glenn, can I ask you something?"

"Sure."

"What would you say if I got Preston and our band back together? I keep trying to tell him we can pick up where we left off, but he says it's too late. What if it's not?"

"It's never too late, Emma. Why do you think I put him in charge of my music department? I knew it'd make him see what he was missing. You just have to show him."

I had some ideas about that. "Thanks, Glenn. I'll see what I can do." We said our goodbyes and I hurried back into the auditorium. Preston was busy talking to the other bands, while John approached me with the biggest smile on his face.

"Thanks for everything, Emma. You have no idea how much this means to me and my band." He hugged me and I watched Preston purse his lips from across the room.

"You're welcome," I replied, letting him go. "You deserve it. But now it's time to get home and pack up. I just got off the phone with Mr. Chandler. He's expecting you early next week. So enjoy your last week in Charleston."

"I can't believe this is happening. The boys are beside themselves. Will you be working with us in Charlotte?"

I shook my head. "Preston will be. I'll be going back to assisting the Chandler's."

"I see," he said, smile fading. "I just want to say, I'm sorry if I overstepped any boundaries before. I didn't realize you were with someone." His gaze found my hand. "You weren't wearing a ring, so I assumed . . ."

"It's okay," I laughed. "No big deal, I promise. I'm sure I'll see you on stage when I get back home."

He winked. "You bet your ass you will."

Once they were gone, Preston approached me, his brows lifted. "The guy just loves to touch you, doesn't he?"

I rolled my eyes. "He was just being friendly. You used to be the same way with women, if I recall correctly."

His gaze darkened. "That was a long time ago. I was stupid."

"Yep. You couldn't see what you had right in front of you."

Pulling me to him, his grip tightened around my waist. "I could see, angel. I just didn't want to fuck it up. You were more to me than just a piece of ass." His lips closed over mine and I melted in his arms.

"It's a good thing you came to your senses," I breathed. "Are you ready to go back to your house?"

Releasing a heavy sigh, he let me go. "Hopefully, we find something today. While you look for the diary, I'm going to see who I can track down, and who's still in the area."

Once everyone left the theater, we hopped in his car and

headed to his house. It would've been easier if they'd had surveillance cameras like Glenn had at his place. Then we could see who broke in.

When we got to the house, I headed straight for Cameron's room, while Preston stayed downstairs on his laptop. Opening Cameron's closet, there were boxes stuffed in the top shelf that contained knickknacks and mementos. The girl also had a ton of shoes too. When I was in high school, I had a couple pairs of dressy sandals and tennis shoes—that was it. I wasn't a fashionable person, and I had never been homecoming queen material either. I was more into sports, like tennis and soccer.

I searched through the boxes and found nothing that would help us. Frustrated, I took a break and sat at Cameron's desk. I'd searched everywhere in her room. The only place I hadn't looked was her bookshelf, but there were only trophies, and a Bible with her name engraved in the brown leather. I never would've pegged the Hale's as a religious family.

Gently picking up the Bible, the weight of it felt off. When I opened it, I realized why. "Holy shit," I gasped low. The whole inside was cut out and another book laid in the middle. I pulled back the cover to the smaller book, and there were pages after pages of what I assumed was Cameron's handwriting. It had to be her diary. Why the hell would she hide it there?

Pulling it out, I opened it up to the first page. It was dated back to her sophomore year, and she talked about how she was nervous about cheerleading tryouts, even though she knew she'd make it. There were entries after entries of typical best friend problems, and how amazing it was when she and Adam finally had sex. I felt like I was intruding on her privacy by reading her personal messages, especially when I got to the entries where she'd written about Preston. They were really close.

Skipping forward, nothing seemed amiss until her senior year of high school. Her writing style had changed, the penmanship aggressive and hard, not the bubbly letters from before. However, I could tell it was still her handwriting.

October 4th

I shouldn't have agreed. How stupid can I be? I've screwed up and there's nothing I can do. If Adam finds out, he'll never forgive me. He'll be mad that I couldn't tell him the truth. What can I do? I can't tell anyone. He says if I don't do what he says, he'll ruin Adam's chances at going pro. I know he's telling the truth. I can't let that happen.

Heart racing, I moved on to another entry.

October 17th

He follows me everywhere. I can sense him even when I can't see him. He's waiting for me to give into him.

He talked about the different ways he'd ruin Adam's career if I ever spoke a word about him to anyone. He scares me.

He says he wants to be with me, to show me what I'm missing. I know it's wrong, but I find myself excited when he's near. A part of me is intrigued that he wants me so bad. I shouldn't be doing what I'm doing, but who can I tell? The way I feel is wrong on so many levels.

November 3rd

I gave in. At school, he cornered me in his secret spot, like he has on so many occasions. Except, this time, touched me under my clothes. It made me feel dirty. I didn't want to like it, but I did. He said as long as I gave myself to him, Adam would be free.

January 14th

We had sex today. When it was over, I thought my payment would be done. But he said we were nowhere near finished. I'm in a lot deeper than I thought.

Months passed by, and I watched the affair unfold right before my eyes. She never said his name, but I knew it was someone she went to school with. The guy had brainwashed her into giving in and it developed into something more. It was a Stockholm syndrome type of situation.

June 12th

Graduation Day. There's a party at Adam's house and everyone's invited, including him. I don't know how to act around him when everyone's around. He finds ways to touch me when no one's looking. I've paid my dues. Any part of me that was excited before has been stifled by fear. I just want my freedom back. There's something about him that scares me.

Adam loves me, and I betrayed him to save him. Some days, I find it hard to look in his brown eyes and not feel disgusted with myself. We want to get married someday. How can I do that with all the lies?

I skipped toward the end.

September 15th

I thought things would calm down once I started college, but they've only gotten worse. Now that I'm not in high school anymore, there's nothing to keep him away. He proved that this summer by trying to get me pregnant. I should've known he wouldn't stop there. I wasn't surprised when he showed up on campus, backing me into an alley between the school buildings.

He says he wants to marry me, even gave me a ring with our initials engraved in it. I didn't know what to do with it, so I rushed back to my dorm and hid it with Skittles. He's lost his mind. I threatened to go to the police if he didn't leave me alone. He laughed in my face. If I go to the police, Adam will find out everything I did. I'll lose him. That's what he wants.

He wants me all to himself.

Preston's footsteps pounded up the stairs and I froze when he entered the room, the diary in my hands. Only, he was too busy looking at his laptop screen to realize what I held.

"I found a couple of guys my sister went to high school with who moved away and came back. I say we find them tomorrow." When I didn't answer, he lifted his head, eyes widening at the sight of the diary. "Did you find it?"

He marched over to me, and knowing I couldn't keep it from him, I let him take it. But when he looked down at it, he laughed, but there was no humor to it. "You know, I thought I'd want to know . . . but I can't bring myself to read it."

"That might be a good thing," I murmured. "I can tell you anything you want to know."

Handing me the diary back, he took one look at my face and knew. "She cheated on Adam, didn't she?" he asked, already knowing the answer. When I nodded, he blew out an angry breath and collapsed on the side of her bed.

"But it's not in the way you think," I rushed to say. "Someone was blackmailing her. She wrote that this person could ruin Adam's football career if she didn't sleep with him. After their first time, she thought it was over, but he wanted more."

His jaw clenched. "Does she say who it was?"

I sat down beside him. "No, but I do know she went to school with him. Apparently, after she graduated, he followed her around, showing up unannounced at her college campus, but there was nothing she could do. If she went to the police, then Adam would've found out what she did. She didn't want to lose him."

"Son of a bitch," he growled. "She could've gone to my father . . . or me. I would've protected her."

"You were only fifteen," I murmured, rubbing his arm soothingly. "You weren't who you are now."

"Does she say anything else?" His voice cracked and it broke my heart.

I could only imagine the effect her words would've had on him if he'd actually read them. "She said this guy gave her a ring, that he wanted to marry her."

"What?" he growled, jumping to his feet. "Are you fucking serious?"

I clutched the diary in my hands. "She said she hid it with Skittles? I'm not sure what that's supposed to mean."

Everything grew quiet as he stared at me in disbelief. "Did you say *Skittles*?"

I nodded. "It's what she said in her last entry." He darted out of the room, and I followed him across the hall. "What are you doing?"

He stormed into his bedroom and threw open his closet door, pushing things around until he got to a box in the corner. Picking it up, he carried it over to his bed, his hands shaking. "Skittles was her favorite stuffed unicorn. I used to make fun of her for sleeping with it. And when she came home one weekend, she gave it to me, wanting me to keep her safe. I never understood why. I just hid it in my closet so my friends wouldn't see it."

Tears fell down my cheeks and I wiped them away. "I can only imagine what your friends would've said if they saw a unicorn on your bed," I teased, hoping to lighten the mood.

He opened the box, and there inside was the white unicorn with rainbow-colored hair. The fur was a little shaggy now, and the white had discolored a bit. We both stared at it, neither one of us ready to make the first move. Preston was a strong man, but even he had limits.

Reaching into the box, I carefully pulled the unicorn out. There was a Velcro tab on the belly, where you could open it up. I could feel something inside.

Preston stepped back, clenching his fists. "Just do it," he commanded.

Taking a deep breath, I opened the flap and reached inside. There was a small, black and red velvet bag, tied off with a red sash. I opened it up and dumped the ring in my hand. It was a single, solitaire diamond set in white gold. Heart racing, I looked inside the band, where two sets of initials stared back at me. I never told Preston they were going to be there.

CRH + NPC

"Preston," I whispered, voice trembling as I showed him the ring. "We have his initials."

Eyes wide, he snagged the ring from my hand. "Holy fuck!" He ran back to Cameron's room and frantically flipped through her yearbook. There was no one in the senior class.

"God-fucking-dammit," he hissed, searching through the juniors and sophomores. "Who the fuck is it?"

He searched and searched, but there wasn't a student with the initials, *NPC*. Tossing the yearbook onto the bed, Preston angrily ran his hands through his hair before ripping his laptop open. "If I have to search for every goddamn person in the area with those initials, I will. I'm not letting this bastard get away."

While he pounded away on the computer, I grabbed Cameron's yearbook and sat down on her bed. "We'll find him," I soothed, searching through the pictures. I made sure to look at every student's face, wondering if any of them could be a killer. "Did Cameron and her boyfriend always hang out with the football players?" I asked.

"Yeah," he growled, huffing as he typed away.

I skipped to the back of the yearbook, where all the sports teams were. There were a lot of guys on the football team, and again, there wasn't anyone with the same initials. *How the hell did we get to a dead end so fast?* That was, until a familiar face caught my attention . . . or at least, he looked familiar. It was hard to tell, since the picture didn't have a close up of his face. His name wasn't listed either.

Dread settled into the pit of my stomach as I flipped through the staff pictures. I wanted to be wrong. However, when I found his picture, I could barely grasp what I saw. "Oh my God," I choked, slapping a hand over my mouth and dropping the book. I felt like I was going to be sick.

I looked over at Preston and shook my head in disbelief.

He looked tense. "What is it?"

"I think I found him. What's worse is—is that I've talked to him."

"I'm sorry, say that again. You've *talked* to him?" he shouted, jumping to his feet.

I nodded, picking up the yearbook again. "At the café. I've run into him twice over the past week." I flipped to the page. Yep, that was him all right.

He grabbed the book, eyes blazing as he stared at the picture. The energy in the room spiked and it made me tremble. I wasn't afraid of Preston, but in that moment, I was terrified.

"He's fucking dead!" Throwing the yearbook across the room, he went back to his laptop, shaking in rage. I'd never seen him so angry.

Coach Nathan Cramer.

I picked the yearbook up off the floor and found Nathan's picture again. He looked young, maybe late-twenties, and very handsome. It made no sense how someone like him would have to blackmail anyone to have sex with him. He could've gotten any girl he wanted.

I had no doubt there were plenty of women who'd fantasized about him. He seemed so normal at the café. "What are you going to do?" I asked cautiously.

Preston pounded away on the computer, then slammed it shut. "The bastard's going down." He stood and stormed out of the bedroom. "Let's go. I have to prepare."

"Wait," I shouted, chasing him out into the hall. "What if he didn't kill her? I mean, yeah, he took advantage of her and deserves to get his dick chopped off, but that doesn't mean he did it."

"Are you fucking serious?" he snapped, eyes wild. Grabbing my arm, he pulled me into his room, yanking out his desk chair. "Sit." I sat down and he showed me his laptop. "Do you see that?" he asked, pointing at the screen.

There were addresses of different cities, all with Nathan's name attached to them. But every couple of years, he found his way back to Charleston to help with the high school football team.

"He moved away after he killed my sister and now he's back again." Squeezing my shoulders, he swiveled me around, gray eyes storming and dangerous. "I have to do this, Emma."

I tried to grab his face, but he pulled away and turned his back on me.

"You can't stop me. I've waited thirteen years for this." His shoulders rose and fell with his rapid breaths.

"I don't want to," I murmured, approaching him cautiously. Placing my hands on his sides, I snaked my arms around his waist. "If this guy killed your sister, I'm all about seeking justice. But there's a reason the police haven't been able to convict him. You can't just go out and kill someone without actual proof."

"It's staring us right in the fucking face," he growled.

I squeezed him harder. "All I'm saying is, let's make *sure* before you go through with this. You'll never be able to live with yourself if you kill an innocent man."

"And how are we going to do that?" He jerked around and stared me in the eyes.

Taking a deep breath, I released it slowly, thinking I was completely insane for what was going through my head. "We do our own investigating," I suggested.

"How?"

A billion things went through my mind, until I realized the simplest and easiest way to do it . . . but that didn't mean Preston was going to like it. It didn't take him long to connect the dots.

"Hell no," he shouted. "No. Fuck that. I'm not letting you anywhere near that fucker."

Huffing, I pushed past him and grabbed one of Cameron's pictures off her dresser. "Look at me, Preston. I might not look like your sister in the face, but the rest of me looks almost exactly like her. If I can remind him of Cameron, it might trigger something. Did all of the other victims look similar to your sister?"

By the look on his face, I got my answer before he even replied. "In one way or another."

"Then all I need are some of her clothes and perfume."

He glared at me like I'd lost my mind. "Do you understand what you're asking me to do? I can't just sit back and watch this guy touch you, when all I want to do is rip out his fucking throat. It's too dangerous."

I shrugged. "But it's all we got. Sure, we could call the police and let them handle it. But if *you* want to catch him, and *you* want to be the one who delivers justice . . . then this'll be the way to do it. Besides, I know you'll be close by. He won't be able to hurt me."

For a split second, I thought he was going to give in, but then the fire ignited in his eyes. "Forget it. You're not doing it and that's final." Charging out of the room, his thunderous steps pounded on the floor and out the back door.

If there was anyone who could make him see reason, it was Glenn. Pulling out my phone, I called his number.

"Emma, you okay?" he answered.

"I'm fine, but Preston's not. I need your help."

"Tell me what you need."

24

PRESTON

My blood boiled. All I wanted was to feel Nathan's bones crack, as I squeezed the life out of him like he did my sister. I wanted justice, but most of all, vengeance. Emma had lost her ever-loving mind if she thought I was going to let her parade around in front of that bastard. There would be other ways to find answers; I just had to figure them out.

My phone buzzed in my pocket and I wasn't surprised to see Glenn's name. "Yeah," I answered.

"You need to let Emma help you."

Clenching my teeth, I breathed in slow. I should've known she'd go to him. "Fuck that," I snapped. "I'll just kill the bastard if I have to."

"In cold blood?"

"It's what I do."

"Not like that, it's not. If Emma can get inside this guy's

head, then let her do it. The sooner she gets in there, the sooner you can make sure he's the guy, and end all of this."

Sighing, I leaned over the railing and closed my eyes. "I don't want her to get hurt. What if something goes wrong?"

"It won't. You'll be there to protect her."

I shook my head, looking at the dunes where we'd found Cameron's body. Rage consumed me. "No," I replied darkly. "She's not doing it."

Glenn blew out an impatient breath. "Do you have another option? If so, please share it with me." With my silence, he continued, "That's what I thought. Fine, I'll drive down there and help her myself. Whether we help her or not, she's doing it. So I suggest you get on board, or I'll be the one protecting her. It's your choice."

"Not if I take her away."

"I'd like to see you try," Emma called out from behind.

I glanced at her over my shoulder, her arms crossed defiantly over her chest.

"She'll be safe with you, Preston," Glenn claimed. "It's time this all came to an end. For your father, before he leaves this world."

Without another word, I hung up and faced Emma, her head held high. She was ready for a fight. I was never one to back down, but she wouldn't forgive me if I forced her away. "I don't like this," I huffed.

Her eyes softened and she sighed. "Neither do I, but I want to help. You can't do this without me." She opened the door and nodded inside. "Please come back. I need you to tell me everything about Cameron you can think of."

I stepped toward her so she could see the seriousness in my eyes. "If we do this, you're going to do exactly what I say, when I say it. Got it?"

She nodded. "Agreed."

"Good. Once we're done here, we have another stop to make before we head home. I hope you're ready for this." I sure as hell wasn't.

The smell of hospitals always reminded me of death. The antiseptic smell only masked what laid beneath. "Want anything from the cafeteria?" Emma asked, squeezing my arm.

I shook my head. "I'm fine. I won't be long. I'll come get you when I'm done."

She kissed my cheek. "Take your time."

I walked her to the cafeteria before hopping onto the elevator. When I got to my father's room, the door opened and the doctor emerged, his face a stony mask.

His head lifted and he spotted me, brows furrowed as he looked at my face. "You must be David's son. I must say, you two look amazingly alike."

I held out my hand. "We get that all the time. How is he?"

He released a heavy sigh. "Not good, I'm afraid. He's gotten worse over the past couple of days. The blood tests show signs of sepsis, which is a common occurrence in patients with pneumonia. It doesn't help that your father's health was already compromised."

"What are you doing to help him?"

"As much as we can," he replied. "We're pumping him full of antibiotics right now but it will only help so much. A lot of damage has been done." He placed a hand on my shoulder. "At this point, we'll move to pain management, and focus on making him as comfortable as possible."

Frozen in place, I watched him walk away. Guilt racked through my body. If I'd only come by sooner, I'd have had more time with my father. Gently opening the door, I walked in, the sound of the machines the only noise in the room. My father's eyes were closed, but they slit open when I sat down beside him.

"I take it you heard the news?" His voice sounded weak and gravelly, but there was no sadness in it.

"I did. And I'm here to tell you to hold on for a little longer."

My father smiled, his eyes getting heavier by the second. "I've been ready to go for a long time now, son. I'm ready to see my wife and daughter again."

Eyes burning, I squeezed them shut. I refused to cry. Crying showed weakness and I couldn't afford that right now. Holding my father's hand, I squeezed it, even though he couldn't feel me. "I know you're ready to see her, but don't you want to hold off until her death is avenged?"

"I don't have time for that, son," he whispered. "Not anymore. My body won't last much longer."

I hovered over him, determined more than ever to catch and kill this guy. "Open your eyes, Dad." Cracking his eyes open, he looked up at me. "Emma and I figured out who killed mom and Cam. I have a name. I'm going after him."

His breath hitched. "How?"

I shook my head, hoping my voice didn't crack. He didn't need to know everything until the deed was done, only that I was going to make damn sure we got our justice. "Doesn't matter. Just hold on until I find him. That way, you can tell mom and Cam when you see them."

A tear fell down his cheek. "I don't know how much longer I have."

I wiped the tear away. "It won't take me long. I promise."

"Then go, son. Do what I couldn't." His eyes closed and I watched him fall asleep.

"I will."

25

EMMA

I could tell there were too many things on Preston's mind when we got home from the hospital. He'd locked himself inside Glenn's gym and pounded away on the punching bag while I ate dinner. There was nothing I could say or do to help him. He was about to lose his father.

Our plan was for me to go to the café and hope he showed up. If he saw me, I could easily strike up a conversation and go from there. Preston and I had already gone through Cameron's things, and I'd taken her perfume, along with a couple of her favorite T-shirts. Preston said she used to wear them all the time. It felt strange knowing I was going to wear her clothes, but if anything could trigger a response from Nathan, it'd be something of hers.

I brought my dishes to the sink and turned around to find Preston standing in the doorway, his body covered in sweat, arms crossed at the chest. I gave him a small smile and he sighed. Walking over, he pulled me into his bare arms, his skin was warm and wet.

"I don't want him touching you, angel. I know what he's going to want from you. He won't be able to resist. Watching you play along is going to fucking kill me."

I placed my hands on his face. "The only man I want touching me is you. You'll just have to stay calm until we can reel him in."

He scoffed. "Easier said than done." Closing his eyes, he blew out an angry breath. "Whatever happens, I'll be close by. You might not see me, but I'll be there."

I leaned up on my toes and kissed him. "I never had any doubt."

Wrapping his arms around my waist, he clutched my shirt in his tight grasp. His warm breath tickled my neck and he bit my skin, sending chills all down my body. "I need you, Emma. I want to fuck you senseless."

I gasped when he bit me again. Disrobing ourselves, we soon stood stark naked in the kitchen—it was a good thing Glenn didn't have any surveillance in the house. My breaths came out so fast, I thought I'd hyperventilate.

He didn't waste any time. Lifting me in his arms, my legs straddled his waist as he carried me up the stairs and into the bathroom. All I wanted to do was slide down on his cock, but he had other plans. Setting me on the counter, I gasped as the cold marble touched my sensitive skin.

Preston turned on the shower, his dark gaze making me tremble. "Oh, the things I'm going to do to you tonight," he growled low. Smirking, he trailed a long, lithe finger over my collarbone and down to my breast. Stopping to circle my nipple, he then trailed down to my aching clit.

Moaning, I arched my back and spread my legs, giving him better access. "I'm going to lose it if you keep touching me, Preston. I'm so close," I cried.

Nipping my ear, he groaned and lightly pushed me back so that my body sprawled out on the bathroom counter. It was so cold against my back, but Preston's warm breath between my legs heated me right up.

"Mmm . . . that's what I like to hear." Getting on his knees, he pulled my butt nearly off the counter so my center would push down on his mouth. Nuzzling me with his nose, he trailed his tongue from my opening on up to my clit. My body jerked from the contact. "You taste so fucking good when you're turned on." He licked me again, and I jerked when he slid a finger inside of me . . . and then another.

Thrusting inside of me, he closed his lips over my clit and sucked while pushing demandingly hard and fast. I exploded all around him, contracting around his fingers as my orgasm spread throughout my body. He slowed his pace and licked me, groaning deep in his chest while getting a taste of what he'd done to me.

"I need you to hold on tight," he growled. Lifting me in his arms, he carried me into the shower and put me right in the path of the shower heads. The water dripped down his dark hair and over his face and body in tantalizing lines.

I wanted to suck him dry, to taste every inch of him. "It's my turn," I said, sliding out of his arms. I bit his lip and sucked hard, trailing a hand down to his arousal. Wrapping my fingers around him, I squeezed, pumping him up and down.

He trembled with my touch and I smiled, keeping my eyes on his as I slowly slid down to my knees to take him into my mouth. Sucking him hard, I moaned and massaged his balls. His head fell back as his fingers gripped my hair, guiding me. I could hear his desire building, grunting as he pushed himself in and out of my mouth.

"Stop, angel. I want to come inside you."

I gave him one last suck and let go with a popping noise, trailing my tongue up his body. It was enough to make him lose control.

Pushing me against the shower wall, he pressed his lips to mine and thrust his tongue inside, lifting me in his arms. He lowered me down on his cock and I cried out, digging my nails into his back.

With his arms under my bent knees, and hands on the wall, he looked down and watched his thick length slide in and out of me. Groaning, he picked up his pace, slamming me down onto him, my back sliding along the wall. Bouncing me a few more times, he lifted me up and set me down on my feet. "I'm going to come if I keep doing that. Turn around and lean your hands against the wall," he commanded, helping me along by pivoting my hips. "Put your leg up on the bench."

I did as he said and leaned against the wall, legs wide apart. Then the tip of his cock grazed my opening before he plunged in deep. Reaching around, he squeezed my breast with one hand, while fondling my clit with the other. In and out he pushed, the friction making my body slide against the slick wall of the shower.

"I want you to come, angel, just like this," he ordered. Groaning, he lowered his fingers to where he could feel his cock gliding in and out of me. When I moaned, he leaned down and bit the side of my neck. "Your pussy is so damn tight. I could fuck you all day long."

Holy hell, he was going to kill me. There were so many sensations triggering my pleasure, I could barely think. I was in pure ecstasy.

When his thrusts became erratic, I clenched my muscles around his cock. "Fuck," he roared, squeezing me harder. "I'm coming." With a roar, he spurt his release inside me.

The deeper he pushed, the faster I succumbed to my release. Screaming, my pleasure fanned out over my body. Breathing hard, I leaned against the wall, trying to catch my breath. Preston was still hard inside me, but he gently pulled out and turned me around to face him.

"Feel good?" he asked, his eyes full of raw heat.

"Oh, yes," I answered breathlessly. "I'm going to sleep good tonight."

Lifting my chin, he nipped me with his teeth. "No you're

not, angel. There's not going to be any sleep tonight."

Pushing his hard cock against my stomach, he looked down at it and then back up to me. "I'm going to make love to you all night long. We don't know what's going to happen tomorrow, or the day after. Right now, you're mine and I need this. I need you."

Shutting off the shower water, Preston opened the door and toweled me off. Guiding me into the bedroom, he pushed me onto the bed, crawling on top of my body.

"You're insatiable," I murmured.

He kissed me on the lips and brought his hand up to cup my cheek. "Only for you." For the longest time, he stared at me, his serious gaze searching mine.

"Everything okay?"

"Yeah," he whispered, brushing the hair off my face. It looked as if he had more to say, but he buried his face into my neck and pushed inside me, his warm breath blowing against my ear as our bodies moved together. "I love you, Emma."

Tears filled my eyes and I held onto him as he made love to me. "I love you too."

26

EMMA

The café was busy, like it was every morning, but there was no sign of Nathan. I ordered my blueberry scone and hot chocolate and took a seat by the window. The sky was clear and the sun glittered across the ocean water. I missed laying out on the beach without a care in the world. Now that the weather was warmer, it was the perfect time.

My phone beeped.

Preston: No sign of him yet.

Me: Ok.

Preston had followed me to the café, but I had yet to see him. He was good at hiding. Glancing at my phone, there was still time for Nathan to show up, since the school didn't start for another forty-five minutes. And if he did, how did I plan on striking up a conversation with him? He was most likely a psychotic killer. Unfortunately, I'd rather him show interest in me than another woman who had no clue what he was.

Another ten minutes passed and I started to lose hope, when my phone beeped again. I didn't have to look to know it was Preston alerting me. It wasn't long before Nathan walked through the door. Averting my gaze, I drew my attention back to the newspaper, pretending I hadn't noticed him. I was hoping he'd come to me. If he truly was the killer, then he'd gotten away with it for over a decade. Meaning, he was a smart man. I didn't want to appear too eager.

Out of the corner of my eye, I could tell he snuck glances at me while he waited for his coffee. My heart raced and I swallowed hard, especially when he walked my way.

"Good morning," he greeted, standing beside my table.

I looked up at him and smiled. "Good morning to you too."

He nodded toward the empty seat across from me. "Is that seat taken?"

"No, not at all," I said, moving my newspaper out of the way. "Have a seat."

Sitting down, he hadn't once taken his piercing green eyes away from me. "Thank you. I don't think we ever exchanged names. I'm Nathan." He held out his hand and I shook it.

"Emma," I replied, releasing his hand. "It's good to meet you."

"Same to you. I was hoping I would get to see you again.

I remember you saying you weren't going to be in town long." He took a sip of his coffee and grinned, flashing his perfectly straight, white teeth.

Nodding, I finished my scone. "I'm going back home in another week or so. My boss said I could take a mini vacation."

"Nice. What do you do for work?"

"I'm a personal assistant. It's not exactly what I thought I'd do with my life, but it's good money. Having a creative writing degree doesn't exactly leave you many choices."

"That's not true," he said in all seriousness. "You could be a teacher, or get a job at a newspaper. I work with a couple of people who have degrees like yours."

"Oh," I said, sounding excited. "Do you work at a newspaper?"

Chuckling, he shook his head. "I'm a football coach at the local high school. I also teach Health Science."

I finished the last sip of my hot chocolate. "That sounds like fun. I bet working with high school students is challenging."

"You have no idea," he said with a smile.

"How long have you been in the school system? You don't look much older than me."

He chuckled again. "And what age is that, twenty-five?"

"No," I laughed. "I'm twenty-seven. You?" I already knew he was pushing forty, but he didn't look like it.

"If I told you, you probably wouldn't be talking to me. I'm sure you have plenty of men your age dying for your attention."

I scoffed. "Please. I haven't had any luck when it comes to

men. Besides, I haven't had time to date. My boss keeps me pretty busy."

"I hate to hear that. Maybe you could find some time to let me show you around town? I don't know how familiar you are with Charleston, but there's a lot to see."

Plastering on a smile, I nodded. "I'd like that. Sounds like fun."

"Great."

I grabbed a pen from my purse and wrote my number down on a napkin. "Here's my cell," I said, handing it to him. "I'm free whenever."

He bit his lip. "How about this afternoon? The team doesn't have practice today, so I could pick you up around four?"

"Perfect."

Looking relieved, he said, "All right, I'll see you then." Glancing down at his watch, he stood. "Unfortunately, I have to go. Class starts in fifteen. But I'll call you this afternoon to get your directions to your place."

"Okay."

He walked out of the café and I watched him disappear around the corner. It wasn't long before Preston texted me.

Preston: He's gone.

I threw away my trash and hurried out to my car so I could call him.

"How'd it go?" he answered.

"Good." Then I cleared my throat. "We have a date tonight."

The thought of being alone with Nathan made me nervous.

The line went quiet. "Doing what?"

"I don't know, he's picking me up around four."

"It's a good thing I put a tracker on his car then. Now I'll know where the cocksucker is at all times."

As much as I hated to admit it, I breathed a sigh of relief. I wasn't looking forward to tonight. "Good. But right now, I want to lay on the beach and get my head straight. I can't believe I'm actually doing this." I was in way too deep.

27

EMMA

The sun felt good on my skin. However, no amount of listening to the ocean waves could ease my tension. I didn't want Preston to know how nervous I was going on the date with Nathan. If he knew, he'd never let me go through with it. Hell, even I had second thoughts. But my worries were assuaged, knowing that Preston would be close by. Even if Nathan was a killer, he had nothing on Preston. Plus, I was strong. If it came down to it, I could fight.

Preston laid beside me on the beach, but I could tell his mind was in a gazillion places. "What are you thinking about?" I asked, propping myself up on my elbow.

He turned to face me, his body mirroring mine. "You don't want to know."

I was pretty sure it involved the myriad of ways he'd like to kill Nathan. But so far, Nathan hadn't exhibited serial killer tendencies. Then again, I didn't know him all that well. I placed my hand on top of Preston's. "Have you thought about where you're going to live when you come to Charlotte?" I asked.

He shrugged. "Not sure."

I bit my lip and smiled. "You could always stay with me for a while, until you get acclimated. Then, if you want, you can get your own place."

"What if you get tired of me?" Grinning mischievously, he grabbed my arm and pulled me on top of him. Luckily, there was no one on the beach.

Giggling, I leaned down and kissed him. "That's not going to happen. I just want you to know you always have a place at my house. I know you don't stay in one place for a long time."

His gaze turned serious. "You're right. Hopefully, we can work around that."

I had to believe we could. He fisted his hands in my hair and bit my lip, before sucking it between his. If we weren't in plain sight, I'd have let him take me right there on the beach. Unfortunately, my phone rang, ruining the mood. I slid off Preston and over to my towel so I could answer my phone.

"Is it him?" Preston asked.

I looked down at my phone, dread settling into the pit of my stomach. "I think so." I didn't have his phone number, but it was a little after three o'clock. School would be out. Taking a deep breath, I blew it out slowly. "Hello," I answered.

"Emma?"

I recognized his voice, all smooth and gentleman-like.

"Hi, Nathan. How are you?"

Preston sat up, jaw clenching as he stared at me.

"Good. Glad to be done with school. Are you still free to go out tonight?"

"Of course. I was just laying out on the beach, hoping to get a head start on my tan before I go home. All I have to do is take a quick shower and throw on some clothes."

"Great, I'm in the same boat. If you give me your address, I'll stop by my house and then head your way."

Preston could hear everything Nathan said. Reluctantly, he nodded. I didn't know if it was a good idea to let Nathan know where I was, but Preston could protect me a lot better there. Besides, it was less than a quarter mile down the road from where Cameron lived.

I gave Nathan the address and the line went quiet. "You still there?" I asked.

"Yeah, yeah, I'm here. I know exactly where you're at. Should be easy to find."

"All right, I'll hurry and get dressed. Do you know what we'll be doing?"

He cleared his throat. "I know of a great place to eat not too far from you. So I thought maybe we could grab a bite and walk across the bridge?"

"Awesome. I'll dress comfortably then." We said our goodbyes and hung up. Preston stood and helped me to my feet. "Hopefully, he doesn't plan on tossing me over the bridge. Other than that, the date seems pretty harmless."

He scoffed. "It better stay that way too. Don't worry though, I'll be close by. And when he drops you off and he's out of the area for good, I'll come to the house. I want to see what he does afterward."

"You don't think he'll make a visit to your house again, do you? He'll obviously see someone's been there."

He nodded. "You're right. But if he *is* the one who broke in, then we have our answer. I'll fuck him up right then and there."

We started toward the house and my steps grew heavy. It was hard to believe it could all come to an end in just a few short hours.

Preston had already left and I was by myself, waiting for the unknown. My phone beeped and my pulse spiked. I was on edge.

Preston: I love you. I'll be close.

Me: I love you too.

Trying to find a murderer wasn't exactly the way I wanted to start off our relationship. Unfortunately, it was the only way I knew he'd be able to move on. I would never completely have him until his family's murderer was brought to justice.

Peeking out the window, a black truck appeared down the street, then turned into the driveway. Nathan hopped out in a pair of khaki shorts and a snug, gray T-shirt that hugged his perfectly sculpted, tan arms. He had an athletic build, like all the other football players I went to high school with.

I didn't want him coming into the house, so I grabbed my purse and ushered myself outside. "Hey," I called out, waving down to him.

He looked up at me and smiled. "Hey, yourself. You ready?"

"More than ready." I locked the door and joined him by his truck. He opened the passenger side door and I hopped inside. "Are we eating first, or walking?"

"Eating," he said with a wink. "That way, if it gets too late, we can walk half the bridge and head back." Once he slid behind the wheel, we were on our way.

"What restaurant are we going to?" I inquired curiously.

A mischievous smile spread across his face. "It's a secret. And when we get there, don't be deceived by the looks of it. It's seriously *the* best place for seafood."

"Where is it?"

He nodded at the road. "On the other end of the island."

When we arrived, the place looked like a dump, but the cars in the parking lot definitely weren't. You could tell the ritzy people in the city ate there. We walked inside and were seated on the back deck, overlooking the water. It was beautiful, making me wish I was there with Preston instead.

"Come here a lot?" I asked.

He shrugged. "When I move back, I do."

"Oh, so you move around a lot?" It was time for some answers. He was about to respond, but then the waitress stopped by to grab our drink orders. I could've used some alcohol for my nerves, but refrained and ordered an iced tea.

"Yeah," he said with a nod. "I have family in New York, Massachusetts, and Virginia. I flip-flop back and forth. Not only does it give me a change of scenery, but I like to move around. Keeps things interesting."

I bet it did. Lots of different high school girls to look at. "Will you be staying in Charleston for a while?" I wondered.

"Probably not. With the school year over next week, I'll head back to Virginia. Then I'll make my rounds again."

The waitress brought our drinks and I surveyed the menu quickly, so I could give her my order. She was a young girl with dark brown hair and a freckled face. Nathan paid her no mind as he ordered his food; his eyes solely on me.

Once I ordered my food, she hurried off to tend to her other tables. It was a packed house. "I'm assuming you don't have close family in Charleston?"

Nathan shook his head. "Only an uncle, but I don't talk to him much. The rest of my family lives in New York, like my mother, father, and so forth. I had a shot at playing pro many years ago, but blew out my knee when I was in college."

"Oh no," I gasped. "That had to be horrible."

"It was. That's why I'm stuck coaching."

"You enjoy it though, right? I'm sure the boys look up to you."

He chuckled. "I hope so. The majority of the teams I coach end up winning championships. That's another reason why I go back and forth, to work with different teams. I go where the money is."

"I see. So the schools are constantly upping their money to get you to work for them?"

Shrugging, his eyes never wavered from mine. "What can I say? I'm that good."

I smiled and took a sip of my tea. "Sounds like it."

"Okay, so enough about me. Where's your family located?"

"In Charlotte," I answered honestly.

"Are you close to them?"

Yes, but I didn't want to tell him that. I needed to make him think I was a loner. That way, no one would miss me too much if I were to up and disappear . . . "Not really. Like I said before, I work *all* the time. It's hard to fit people into my schedule." Our food came and my shrimp smelled heavenly, all butter and garlic.

"That's a shame," Nathan said. "Do you think maybe you could work on that?"

I took a bite of my shrimp. "What do you mean?"

"I mean," he said, staring at my mouth while I chewed. "Do you think you could fit me in when you go back home? I'd like to keep in touch with you. It's been a long time since I've met anyone who can keep my interest."

"You must not get out very often," I teased.

"Oh, I do, but I have particular tastes."

I'll bet he did.

Nathan paid for dinner and we were on our way to the bridge. The sun was still out and we had about three more hours before it'd be completely dark. I wanted to be done with our walk way before then.

The bridge had walking paths so people could enjoy the bridge without having to worry about sharing the road with cars. The only thing I didn't like was feeling it shift under my feet. Bridges made me nervous. Every time I drove over one, I always lowered my windows so that if my car fell into the water, I'd have an escape.

Nathan walked alongside me, our arms touching periodically. "How long have you been single?" he asked.

"Too long." I laughed. "Don't get me wrong, I've dated here and there, but nothing serious. You?" I looked over at him and he shrugged.

"That's kind of the same thing for me. I got burned once, a long time ago."

"Uh-oh, that's not good. I think everyone's gotten hurt by someone at some point in their lives. In fact, my ex left me for another woman," I said, hoping to see a spark of something on his face. But he just shook his head.

"What a fucking idiot. Any man would be stupid to give you up." He glanced down at my hand and clasped it in his. It felt weird, walking hand in hand with another man. There was no way I was going to be able to walk the rest of the way like that.

We stopped halfway across the bridge and I let his hand go so I could place them on the railing. It was for the best. If Preston was close, he'd be fuming by this point. However, the view across the water was incredible. When I turned to face Nathan, he couldn't take his eyes off me.

"You are absolutely beautiful," he murmured, stepping closer. "I don't know what it is about you, but I haven't been able to stop looking at you."

"Thank you." I looked down briefly, pretending to be bashful. "You're not so shabby yourself."

He smiled. "Is it bad that I want to see you again?"

"No," I laughed. "I'll take it as a compliment."

He reached out his hand and brushed a strand of my hair behind my ear.

It took all I had not to recoil from his touch. The man could be innocent, but it still didn't change the fact I was letting another man touch me.

"You remind me of someone," he whispered.

"Who?"

Then it was as if he snapped back into reality. "Nobody," he answered with a shake of his head. "Are you about ready to head back to my truck? I don't think we'll get the full six miles in tonight."

"I'd say not." I chuckled.

He gently took my hand and we walked back to his truck.

The sun set as we drove home. And the darker it got outside, the more my nerves frazzled. I hoped he didn't want to prolong the night.

It didn't take long to get back to my house, and when we did, he got out of his truck to walk me to my door. *Please don't ask to come in.*

"I had fun tonight, Emma," he said, putting his hands in his pockets.

There was something about his crystal green eyes that made me tremble. It was like he could see right through me, or maybe that was me being paranoid. At least he wasn't going to try and touch me. "I did too," I replied.

"I know it's awfully quick, but would you mind if I saw you again tomorrow?"

"Sure. You could always come over and I'll cook you dinner? That way I can pay you back for tonight." I could have Mrs. Walker make it and pretend I did it.

"You don't have to do that. But if you want me to come, I will."

"It's a date then," I said, putting on a smile.

Closing the distance, he released his hands from his pockets and I froze as he placed them on my hips. His lips came close to mine, but instead, he pressed them to my cheek. "Sweet dreams, Emma."

"Goodnight," I murmured back.

He walked down to his truck and opened his door. "Will you be at the café in the morning?"

I nodded. "Of course. You know I can't live without my hot chocolate."

"Good deal. I'll be there too."

I waved and he got in his truck and drove away. It wasn't long before my phone buzzed in my back pocket. I pulled it out, not surprised to see Preston's name. "Hey," I answered.

"Do you have any idea how hard it was to watch that shit?"

I blew out a sigh. "Not as hard as it was to endure it. Where are you?"

"Making sure that fucker heads as far away from the house as possible. I'll be there soon."

"Good. I'll be waiting."

28

PRESTON

Watching that bastard touch Emma was the hardest fucking thing I had to do. I knew he was guilty. You could see it in his soulless eyes. Those hands that held Emma's were the same ones that took the life from my mother and sister. The thought made me sick to the core. Some days it was hard to contain the rage and today was one of them.

There was a look every demented person had, and Nathan had it in spades. If only I could get away with killing the fucker before he tried to hurt Emma. Unfortunately, she was too goddamned stubborn to see the monster right in front of her.

I made sure to put enough distance between my car and Nathan's as I followed him off the island. I'd hoped he would go by my house so I could end it, but he didn't. Instead, he drove to his Mt. Pleasant home and parked for the night. With the tracker I had on his vehicle, I'd be able to see where he was at all times, getting alerts when his truck moved.

It was getting late, so I headed back to Glenn's house, making sure to park down the road in case fuckhead decided to drive by in the middle of the night like the stalker I knew he was.

Walking around to the back of the house, I opened the door. The kitchen lights were on, but everywhere else in the house was dark. "Emma?" I called out. No response. I stopped at the staircase and looked up into the darkness, catching the faint flicker of candlelight coming from her bedroom.

I took the steps two at a time and slowly walked toward her room. When I entered, I found her on the bed, completely naked.

"It's about time you got here," she whispered, biting her lip.

My dick twitched, as the anger I harbored inside morphed into lust. I knew what she was doing. She knew I'd be livid about tonight. "What are you doing, angel?"

She slid to the edge of the bed and beckoned me closer. I moved toward her and she unbuttoned my jeans, sliding them down to the floor. I tore off my shirt and groaned as she massaged me like a pro, her tongue sliding across the tip of my cock. Eyes rolling into the back of my head, I moaned. I was close to losing control, when she stopped and trailed her tongue up my stomach.

"I want you inside of me," she demanded, biting my chest.

This was exactly what I needed.

Ten minutes later, I pulled out from her warm center and

rested on my elbow so I could look down at her. So many emotions swarmed through my body; I didn't know what to feel. I sure as hell didn't want to be angry all the time, and thankfully, she helped with that. Only, it never lasted for long. There was too much bad shit to pull me back under.

"We need to talk," I said in all seriousness.

Her smile faded. "I was hoping to get your mind off everything."

I brushed a finger across her lips. "Trust me, angel, making love to you helps, but what we're doing is serious. You don't see what I see. I deal with sick bastards on a daily basis. It only takes one thing to make them snap. Cramer might not be there yet, but he's never very far from that line."

"How do you know?"

I couldn't help but admire her innocence. I didn't want it taken away from her. She saw the good in the world, whereas all I saw was the bad. She was the perfect balance to me. "It's in his eyes, Emma. I don't know, maybe I'm jaded, but I can see the evil that goes on in this world. We need to push him, to get him to crack."

Her brows furrowed. "How are we going to do that?"

Visions of my sister flashed through my mind. "We need to turn you into Cameron. Make him see her when he looks at you. If there's going to be a trigger, that'd be it. We have to mentally fuck him up. He'll eventually reach a breaking point. The sooner, the better."

"Then I guess I can start tomorrow. He's coming over for

dinner."

"What?" I growled.

She cringed. "I figured it'd be better than going over to *his* house. Plus, if he's going to try and do something, it'd be when we're alone. Honestly, I don't know if he's the guy we're looking for."

That was the innocence that could get her in trouble; and also what scared me. "Oh, he's the one all right, and we'll prove it. But being here doesn't make me feel any better. Being in public protects you. I'm not ready to put you in harm's way."

She kissed me, her lips soft and warm. "There's no other option. I'll be fine, I promise. I just need you to coach me on everything Cameron. I know it won't be easy, but if you have videos of her, that would help more than anything."

There were a lot of home videos back at the house. Although, I didn't know if I was ready to watch them. "Okay," I agreed. "We'll get to work tomorrow."

29

EMMA

Preston followed me to the café, like he'd done the day before. Nathan was already inside, sitting at the same table. He smiled like any gentleman would do when I walked in. I waved and ordered my hot chocolate before joining him.

Leaning over the table, he kissed me on the cheek. "Good morning. You look beautiful as always."

I waved him off. "You're just saying that because I'm cooking your dinner tonight."

"And what are we having?" he asked, his voice low and seductive. If I was single and didn't know of his past, I could see myself getting sucked under his spell.

"Meatloaf, mashed potatoes, and green beans. It's my favorite." Well, it'd had been Cameron's favorite meal. Not that it was an iconic dinner to make him remember her, but it was a start in the right direction.

"Sounds good. Do I need to bring anything?"

I shook my head. "Just yourself. Then maybe after dinner we could take a walk on the beach?"

"I look forward to it," he said, smiling as he glanced at his watch. "Dang it. I gotta go. We have a staff meeting this morning."

"Fun." I laughed. "I'll be thinking of you as I enjoy the rest of my hot chocolate and a day out on the sand."

He winked. "Maybe one day I'll get to join you."

"Maybe."

Tossing his cup in the trash, he smiled at me once again before walking out the door.

"Hey, Emma," a voice called out.

I turned to the voice and watched John walk toward me. "Good morning," I greeted happily. "Are you and the band all ready for Charlotte?"

He sat down at the table and laughed. "For the most part. We're leaving tomorrow." He looked at the front door before continuing, "I'm not taking your boyfriend's spot am I?"

I choked on my drink and coughed. "No, not at all. He's not my boyfriend. Nathan's a friend from around here."

"Ah, I see. That explains why he was staring at you that one day."

Frozen, I stared at him in confusion. "What are you talking about?"

He sipped his coffee and pointed at the tree just outside. "Remember the day I told you someone was staring at you, and when you turned around he was gone?"

"Yeah." Dread settled into the pit of my gut. Glancing over at the tree, I remembered thinking it was Preston at the time. "Are you saying it was Nathan?"

He nodded. "I thought he was your boyfriend."

My palms grew sweaty and I felt sick. Had Nathan really been watching me *before* our plan to out him? If so, it changed things drastically.

"Emma, you okay? You look pale." John placed his hand on mine.

Not even finishing the rest of my drink, I got up and threw it in the trash, trying my best to plaster on a smile. "I'm sorry. I forgot I'm late for a meeting. I hate to run out on you, but I have to go. Be careful on your way to Charlotte. I'm sure I'll see you around next week."

"I sure hope so."

I waved, then bolted out the door to my car. Once I was on the road, I called Preston.

"Everything okay?" he asked. "You ran out of there kind of fast."

"No," I choked, swallowing hard. "I think you might be right."

"About Nathan?"

"Yeah. I ran into John in the café, and told me something that disturbed the hell out of me."

"What is it?"

My heart raced and I felt like I was going to throw up.

"Remember when I accused you of stalking me? John was the one who pointed it out to me. Can you take a guess as to who it was?"

"Fuck me," he growled. "There's no telling how long he's been watching you."

"Exactly. What if he's seen us together?"

He sighed. "Then it'll be even more like his scenario with Cameron."

"And it drove him over the edge when she chose Adam over him," I added. "If he knows I'm leading him on, he hasn't given any indication as such."

Preston huffed. "Let's just hope he doesn't. Either way, he chose you. We just have to ride it out as planned."

Knowing Nathan had been watching me since before we'd figured everything out, scared the shit out of me. Maybe I *was* wrong about him. The phrase 'looks can be deceiving' crossed my mind.

I spent the afternoon looking through Cameron's pictures, and watching home videos. She had been intelligent, vivacious, and naturally beautiful. One would have never thought she was being blackmailed at the time the videos were made. It was like she led a double life. If only she'd had the courage to get help before she got sucked in.

Preston could only watch for so long, before he had to walk away. I hoped that once we caught the killer he'd be able to move on, that the pain would lessen. But even then, he still had his father to worry about. Preston was a bomb ready to explode, and there was nothing I could do about it.

Mrs. Walker was downstairs cooking the meatloaf, while I braided my hair to the side, watching myself in the mirror as I turned into Cameron. Preston had said it was how she loved to wear her hair. We wore the same size clothes, which worked out perfectly. Her shirt was a little snug around my breasts, but it was her favorite—a Green Day T-shirt she had gotten at one of their concerts.

Preston stood by the window, his face a stone-cold mask. I knew it was hard for him to talk about Cameron all day. "I need to leave soon," he murmured.

I walked up behind him and put my arms around his waist. "Where will you be?"

"Just outside. Make sure you stay in sight. If you don't, I'll have no choice but to come in."

I nodded. "I can do that. I plan on staying downstairs, then going for a walk."

Turning around, he finally looked at me for the first time since I put on Cameron's clothes. "She loved that shirt," he murmured. "None of her friends were into Green Day, so I went with her to the concert. It was one of the best nights I had with her."

I remembered seeing a picture of them at the concert, wearing the exact same shirt. "You were a good brother, Preston. She and your mother would be proud of you."

He scoffed. "Don't know about that."

"Well, I am, if it counts for anything," I said, holding his face in my hands. "I love you."

Releasing a heavy sigh, he kissed me. "I love you too. Be careful tonight."

"I will."

Hurrying past me, he marched down the stairs and out the front door. The house smelled amazing and when I joined Mrs. Walker in the kitchen, the food was already done. "You sure you don't need me anymore tonight?" she asked.

I waved her off. "I'll be fine. Go spend time with your hubby. I know your anniversary's coming up this weekend. I'm sure I can manage on my own for the next couple of days."

Her eyes widened. "You sure?"

Chuckling, I hugged her tight. "Yes, now go. Have a good night." Grabbing her belongings, she strolled out the door with a smile on her face.

My phone beeped with an incoming text.

Nathan: On my way.

Me: Dinner is ready. :)

A few minutes later, he pulled into the driveway. I waited for him to get to the door before I opened it. When I did, he stood stock still, gaze roaming slowly over the length of my body. He looked like he'd seen a ghost. *Perfect.*

"You look . . ."

I waved him in and hugged him tight, hoping Cameron's perfume would waft to his nose. "I know, I'm sorry. You're all spiffed up and I look like a hobo. I was hoping to change clothes, but I didn't have time," I said, running a hand down my braid, feigning embarrassment.

Shaking his head, he cleared his throat and breathed me in. "No, it's fine. Honestly, I'm shocked to see you're a Green Day fan."

"Really?" I replied, letting him go. "They were one of my favorite bands growing up. I got it at a concert."

He stared at me as if I was a completely different person. His hand lifted and he touched my braid, running his fingers over my hair. "I love it when you wear your hair like this," he murmured.

I'd never worn my hair like that, but I didn't correct him. "Thanks. I like it too. It stays out of my way. You ready to eat?"

My braid slid threw his fingers and I moved away, pulse racing as sweat ran down my back. He wouldn't stop staring at me, which made me more nervous than I ever had been. I nodded toward the kitchen and he followed me. There were two place settings at the table, so I grabbed our plates and handed him one.

"Get as much as you want." The food smelled amazing, but the bundle of nerves in my gut was working hard to make sure I wasn't hungry. Still, I loaded up my plate and sat down at the table, where Preston could see us. "Want any lemon with your tea?" I asked him.

Taking a bite of his food, he looked at me and shook his head. "I'm good."

There was a basket of lemons and limes on the counter, so I got up and grabbed a lime. Preston had told me how Cameron loved to put lime in her tea, that her family always made fun of her for it. I personally didn't like the taste of anything in my tea, but I was committed to being Cameron, so I chopped it up and carried a couple of slices over to the table, squeezing them into my glass.

Nathan swallowed hard. "You put lime in your tea?"

I laughed. "I know it's weird, but it's good. You should try it sometime."

"I think I'll leave that to you," he said with a small smile.

Throughout dinner, I tried not to notice him gawking at me, but it was hard. I kept my focus on my food and tried to pretend he wasn't there. Unfortunately, that was hard as hell to do. "What are you going to do for summer vacation?" I hedged, attempting to take the focus away from me for a while.

He cleared his throat. "Hopefully, spend some of it with you."

"Are you going to drive down to see me? My work schedule will be kind of hectic."

"I don't care. I can't go all summer without seeing you. I'll drive anywhere to be with you, you should know that."

I smiled, but there was nothing that came out of my mouth. The things he said were strange, so I played along. We didn't know each other well enough for him to drive anywhere in the world for me. I finished my food and put all the dirty dishes in the sink. The house felt like it was closing in around me, or maybe it was because Nathan was coming up behind me. I could see his reflection in the microwave.

"Want to get some fresh air?" I asked, turning around to face him. He nodded and stepped back, letting me walk past to the patio door. I breathed a sigh of relief the second I felt the wind hit my face.

Nathan came up behind me, his arms wrapped securely around my waist. I could feel his warm breath on my neck as he bent down to kiss my skin. Chills ran down my arms and I fought my instinct to recoil.

Needing my space, I attempted to start a conversation. "Where did you grow up?"

He kissed my neck again, breathing me in deeply. I knew he could smell Cameron's perfume this close up. "Here and there, mainly in Virginia. I have a cabin up there. You should come see it. I prefer the beach though."

I had to think about everything Preston told me about his sister. There had to be something else I could say. With him touching me, I couldn't think straight. All I wanted was to push him off and run away. Peering out at the water, I concentrated on the waves and my breathing. Then something came to mind. "Have you ever tried to surf?"

He chuckled and I could feel the vibration against my back; he was too close. "All the time. I wasn't very good at it though. Football was the only sport I ever excelled at."

There was a patio chair turned over, so I stepped out of his hold to fix it. It was the perfect opportunity to gain some distance. "I tried surfing one time."

His brows lifted and he smiled. "Oh yeah?"

"Yep, I ended up getting stung by a jellyfish. It especially sucked because I had a cheering competition not long afterward. My parents made me bathe in vinegar. I smelled like a tossed salad for a damn week. I refused to go to school, it was so bad."

His smile faded. "How old were you?"

I looked right into his eyes. "Seventeen. I was a senior in high school." It was all a lie, but it was during the time he was intimate with her. Surely, he'd remember. "Anything like that ever happen to you?" I added.

"No," he murmured, placing his hands on my face. His eyes darted back and forth between mine. "It's strange, but I feel like I've known you before."

Desperation showed across his face and I took advantage of the moment. "I feel the same way," I whispered. "I'm a firm believer in reincarnation. Maybe we were together in another life?"

Sucking in a ragged breath, his grip tightened and he moved closer. "Do you really think it's possible?"

I wrapped my hands around his wrists and squeezed, leaning into him. "When two people are meant to be together, they always find their way back, one way or another." Now *that* I truly believed in.

The smile that spread across his face made me shiver—possessive and feral. It was almost as if he was a different person. "Could it really be?" He wasted no time, moving in to press his lips to mine. When he deepened the kiss with his tongue, I tried to pull back, but his grip was too tight. Wrapping his arms around my waist, his erection pressed against my leg. "I need you, Cameron," he whispered, sliding his hand under my shirt.

Hearing her name terrified me. "Stop," I shouted, panic overtaking me. I pushed him off and stepped back. His chest rose and fell with rapid breaths, the air thick with his lust. "I'm not ready to go that far, not when I'm leaving in a couple of days."

My reaction snapped him back to reality. Eyes wide, he stumbled into the railing. I had no clue if he realized he'd called me Cameron or not. "I'm so sorry. I don't know what came over me," he replied desperately, tearing his eyes away from mine. "I should go."

Without another word, he charged into the house and grabbed his keys off the counter, before disappearing out the front door. I heard tires screech as he tore out of the driveway. It wasn't long before Preston raced up to the deck, pulling me into his arms.

"You okay?"

Swallowing hard, tears fell down my cheeks. I hadn't realized how hard it would be to play along. "No. I feel dirty. I don't think I can do this anymore." I felt safe in his arms and I didn't want to let go.

"Good. I can't stand watching that bastard touch you. It took all I had not to rip him off you and snap his neck."

Burying my head in his chest, I cried. "He called me Cameron."

His body tensed. "I'm gonna follow him. Will you be okay?"

Nodding, I let him go. "Go. I'll be fine."

He took off and I was left there, alone with the sound of the waves. My skin felt like spiders were crawling all over me and I couldn't get away from the smell of Nathan's cologne. I needed a shower to wash it all away.

30

PRESTON

nraged couldn't begin to cover the way I felt. After tonight,
I would never let Emma anywhere near Cramer again.
Knowing he'd called her Cameron sealed the deal. I'd have
to find another way to prove his guilt.

It took a while to catch up to Nathan and when I did, I
saw his truck parked in the parking lot of an abandoned
warehouse. Nathan was still in his truck, with his head resting
on the steering wheel. I slowed my vehicle and turned down
the opposite street. It was dark with no streetlights, which
worked in my favor. I found a place to park and snuck through
the trees with my rifle slung across my shoulders.

At first, Nathan kept his head on the steering wheel,
completely still, but then all hell broke loose. Pounding his fists
against the wheel, he let loose a string of profanities, yelling at
the top of his lungs. When he got out of the truck, he kicked

his door and slammed his hands down on the hood. The look on his face was sheer panic . . . and rage. I could feel it in my blood—he was the one.

Taking a deep breath, I got into position on the ground. I could see Nathan through my scope, leaning over on the hood of his truck. I had the perfect shot. He didn't deserve a fast death, but if it stopped him from going after Emma, I'd make the sacrifice.

I breathed in and let it out. *One.* I did it again. *Two.* Finger on the trigger, I was ready to pull, when my phone vibrated in my pocket. *Fuck.* I thought I could ignore it, but then it buzzed again and again. Clenching my teeth, I pulled it out of my pocket. It was Emma.

I stared at the phone, then back at Cramer, who'd gotten back into his truck already. I'd missed my chance. He drove away and I rushed back to my car. If he was going toward Emma, nothing was going to stop me from killing him. Once in my car, I tracked his route, only to find him heading away from Emma. A part of me was relieved, but the other part wanted another chance to put him down.

Pulling out my phone, I called Bryce, the only Chandler son who didn't get on my nerves. "What's up, Hale?" Bryce answered, his voice serious.

"I need you to do me a favor. Can you drive down and take Emma back to Charlotte? She's not safe here."

"What's going on? Do you need help?" he asked.

"It's nothing I can't handle. I just don't want her in the

crossfire. Once she's gone, I can do what I need to do."

"All right, I'll be there tomorrow night."

"Good deal. See ya then." We hung up and I breathed a sigh of relief. Emma was going to be furious, but if I told her to go on her own, she wouldn't leave. She was the most stubborn woman I knew.

Emma called again and this time I answered it. "Hey."

"Where are you?"

"On my way back."

The line grew silent. "Did you . . . do it?"

If she only knew how close I was to pulling the trigger. "No, but you're leaving tomorrow."

"What?" She gasped. "Why?"

"The guy's truly fucked up in the head. He's going to blow any day now, and I don't want you anywhere near him."

"You can't make me leave. I need to stay with *you*."

She was afraid I'd lose myself again. I could see it on her face every time something bad happened. "I'll be fine, Emma. I can't do my job if I'm constantly worried about you. It's for the best."

"I'm not leaving," she huffed.

"You are," I said, releasing a heavy sigh. "You have no choice."

By the time I got back to Glenn's house, I wasn't surprised to see Emma by the door, standing defiantly with her arms crossed. She stormed out and shouted, "You're not making me leave, Preston Hale."

How was I going to make her understand? I walked up the stairs and stopped in front of her. "Bryce is coming to take you back to Charlotte," I informed her.

Her mouth fell open. "You can't be serious. How could you do this to me?"

Taking her arm, I pulled her inside and shut the door. "Because I need you in my life. Which means, I want you far away from here until that psychotic fuck has been dispatched. You didn't see what I saw tonight. Cramer lost his shit, and it's only a matter of time before he comes after you."

She threw her arms in the air. "He's not going to, if I'm gone. You'll be back at square one."

I shook my head. "I don't need him to break any further. I've already got the proof I need. And I can't do my job effectively while worrying about you. I might make a mistake."

"I can take care of myself," she backfired. "Please, Preston. Don't make me go. I don't want to leave you."

Turning on my heel, I went into the kitchen and she followed, only I kept my back to her. "You're going to leave tomorrow, even if Bryce has to take you, kicking and screaming."

Grabbing my arm, she tried to turn me around, but her strength was no match for mine. I knew she was strong, but she wouldn't be able to fight off a man like Nathan for long. I turned around and faced her.

"You need to trust me in this. He had a psychotic breakdown, Emma. That might not scare you, but it's not something to play around with. You don't know the kind of shit I've seen. I've seen horrors that no one would ever think possible. And *you* are the only thing in my life that gives me hope." Tucking a strand of her hair behind her ear, she leaned into my touch. "I can't lose you, angel. It'd be the end of me." I kissed her and closed my eyes, fighting back my own tears. "I love you so fucking much. I wish you knew."

Collapsing in my arms, she held me tight, crying softly against my chest. "I love you too. That's why I don't want to leave you."

I kissed the top of her head. "You'll see me again soon, I promise. Besides, we still have tomorrow."

31

EMMA

Before going downstairs the next morning, I packed my clothes and called my parents to let them know I was coming home. My mother promised to make spaghetti, since she hadn't seen me in weeks. I couldn't wait to see them. Knowing Preston was about to lose his father made me appreciate having my parents even more. I didn't want to take for granted the time I had with those I loved.

When I found Preston in the kitchen, he'd already cooked breakfast. "Smells good," I said, watching the muscles in his back ripple every time he moved.

He glanced at me over his shoulder and smiled. "Sit down and I'll make you a plate." The plate he set down in front of me was filled with eggs, bacon, and grits. My stomach growled and I ate every bite of it before he even sat down to join me. He looked at my empty plate and laughed. "Hungry much?"

I wiped my mouth off with a napkin. "Hey, I went to bed hungry last night. Then *you* went ahead and banged me six ways from Sunday. I needed the nourishment."

He chuckled and I loved the sound. "I can make you more."

"Nah." I gave a wave of my hand. "I'm good. Thanks though."

"What do you want to do today?" he asked. "Bryce should be here around four."

I looked out the window and smiled; the weather was beautiful. "We could go for a walk and hang out. I don't mind being lazy today. I know you won't be able to relax once I'm gone." Not until he could convict Nathan of murdering his family.

He sighed. "You're right. I'll be working twenty-four-seven."

"What if Nathan doesn't do anything?" I inquired. "Are you going to keep after him?" His gaze found mine and I could see right through him. He was going to get rid of Nathan, no matter what evidence he found, or didn't find. He started to answer, but I held up my hand. "Stop. Don't say anything. It might be best I don't know."

"Agreed," he grunted. Finishing up his food, Preston reached for my empty plate. "Heard anything from him this morning?"

I glanced down at my phone. "Not yet. And it's Saturday— he doesn't have school. Maybe I freaked him out too much last night?"

He scoffed. "Doubt it. He'll call. And when he does, you need to end it. If he gets mad, I'll be right here."

"That's what you want, isn't it? You want me to piss him off to the point he does something stupid."

"I told you," he said, placing the dishes in the sink, "he's going to blow. And when he does, you'll be gone and I'll be ready."

"Will you call me every now and then to let me know you're okay?"

Closing the distance, he wrapped his arms around my waist, lifting me up onto the counter. I held him tight as he kissed me. "Yes, I promise. You're not the only one who's going to suffer in this."

I deepened the kiss and closed my eyes, relishing in his touch. His stubble tickled my neck as he kissed his way down the column of my throat. My whole body was sore from the night before, especially at my core. It didn't matter though. I needed him.

"Make love to me," I moaned, nipping his ear.

Without warning, he picked me up and carried me out of the kitchen. But we didn't get far before my phone rang. Preston froze, his gaze darkening with each ring. "Think it's him?" he asked, setting me down.

My heart raced. "Don't know." I hurried over to the kitchen table and grabbed my phone. "It's Nathan."

Preston's fists clenched and he huffed. "Might as well get it over with. It needs to end."

Swallowing hard, I accepted the call, hoping like hell my voice didn't crack. "Hello?"

"Emma, it's Nathan."

I licked my dry lips. "Hey, are you okay? You left in such a hurry last night."

Nathan sighed. "I know. I'm sorry about that. Is there any way I can make it up to you?"

"Unfortunately, I don't see how. I'm getting ready to go home."

A small silence passed before he replied. "But I thought you had a couple more days?" The sound of his voice gave me chills. He was angry.

"I'm so sorry. Something came up at work and my boss asked me to come back early. It was nice meeting you though. Maybe I'll run into you again next time I'm in town?"

He scoffed. "Really. That's *it*? You don't have time to see me before you go? I thought we had a connection."

"We did," I lied, "but I've never had any luck with long-distance relationships, and I'm not sure when I'll be back in Charleston. I can call you the next time I'm in the area, but it's probably best we end it for now."

"Is this because of what happened last night? I said I was sorry. I didn't mean to come on too strong."

I looked up at Preston and he waved me on to finish it. "Oh, no, that has nothing to do with it. It's okay, Nathan. Really. I'm not upset with you. I just don't think we're going to work out this time around. Maybe later. I'm so sorry. I wish you all the best. Goodbye." I hung up the phone before he could say anything else.

Preston took my phone and shut it off. Hopefully, there wouldn't be a bunch of messages and texts when I turned it back on. It was like high school all over again, only *this* boyfriend might be a serial killer.

"You did good, angel. It's over."

My chest ached. "Doesn't feel like it."

Putting his arm around me, he led me to the back door and we walked outside. "Let's go for a walk. Maybe we can hop in the pool when it warms up."

"Make sure to bring your tracker with. I don't want that guy sneaking up on us."

"Got it covered." He showed me the app on his phone.

"Okay then. Let's do it."

Halfway through our walk on the beach, Preston's phone alerted us. It wasn't a text or a call . . . it was letting him know that Nathan was on the move. He pulled out his phone, expression guarded.

My stomach clenched and I felt sick. What if he was coming for me? I wasn't ready to deal with this shit. "Where's he going?" I asked.

His brows furrowed as he looked at the screen. "Northwest. He's on the highway, headed toward Columbia."

"Really? I wonder where he's going?" If he was headed to

Columbia, he could easily keep going until he got to Charlotte. Dread settled into the pit of my stomach. "Oh my God. What if he's going to Charlotte?"

Preston's jaw clenched. "If that motherfucker's headed there, then you're gonna stay here with me. We'll keep a watch on him and change our plans accordingly."

"Do you think you should follow him? I don't want him hurting anyone."

By the look on his face, he was worried about that too. "No, not at this point." He slid the phone back into his pocket. "I'm not leaving you to chase him. I have plenty of time for that when you're gone. Although, I do want to stop by my house later on to look around. I'm beginning to think it's time to pack up some of their belongings."

That was a huge step for him. In the multiple times we'd been to his house, he had never even attempted to go into his parents' room. I couldn't imagine how hard it was going to be. Taking his hand, I squeezed it tight. "I'll help you."

He shook his head. "I don't want us spending our last day doing that."

"It's okay. I can at least help you get started."

Lifting our clasped hands, he gently kissed mine. "What would I do without you?"

"Hopefully, miss me," I laughed. "I did see some boxes in Glenn's garage. I'm sure he wouldn't mind if we used them to pack up the stuff. Might as well get started. Besides, maybe we'll run across something we missed."

32

EMMA

For the past couple of hours, Preston and I worked on Cameron's room, packing up her belongings. We were going to need more boxes than we had. "What are you going to do with all of her stuff?" I asked.

He carefully packed away the last of Cameron's trophies. "Put most of it in storage. Her clothes I can donate. Not unless you want to keep some of them?"

I remembered the Green Day shirt and how it was special to both him and Cameron. "I'd like to keep her favorites, if you don't mind. You wouldn't want to get rid of those."

He glanced at me over his shoulder, his gaze full of sadness. "You're right."

An hour later, her room was almost packed up, as far as clothes went, but I still had one of her dressers to go through. Other than that, all she had was furniture . . . and the two most important things.

Her diary sat on the bed, along with Skittles and Nathan's ring. "What are you going to do with her diary and the ring?"

With a heavy sigh, Preston taped up the box of trophies. "We need to keep them safe and as far away from Cramer as we can, until everything's over. We'll need it all for evidence." He walked over and picked them up, handing them to me. "I need you to take these with you."

I held them to my chest. "You sure? Skittles is supposed to be yours to keep safe."

A sad smile spread across his face. "Cameron won't mind. If it wasn't for you, we never would've had this lead."

"I'll guard them with my life." My stomach chose that moment to growl, causing his smile to widen.

"Hungry?"

I snorted. "It's been hours since we ate breakfast. Of course I'm hungry."

Brows furrowed, he pulled out his phone. The last time we'd checked on Nathan's whereabouts, he was in Columbia. We had no clue if he was going to head back down or go north toward Charlotte. It was a waiting game.

"Why don't we take a break and grab some lunch at the house? I can make us some sandwiches," he offered.

"Or you could always make them and bring 'em back here? I just have one more dresser to pack up. Once I'm done with it, this room will be finished and we'll have plenty of time to do *other* things before I leave. Plus, we need more boxes," I added.

He bit his lip and pulled me in close. "Sure you'll be okay?"

I rolled my eyes. "I'll be fine." My stomach growled again and I clutched it. "Hopefully."

Chuckling, he kissed me quick and disappeared down the stairs. "I'm locking the door behind me," he shouted from below.

"Okay," I hollered back.

The sun shone through the window and I opened it, letting the salty sea air blow freely through the room. It was two o'clock and the beach was vacant. It was nice not seeing the sand covered with tourists. I wasn't a local, but I hated crowded beaches.

It didn't take long to pack up the last dresser full of clothes. Taking a break, I grabbed Cameron's diary and sat down on her bed. There were so many entries, it'd take me hours to look through them all, but there had to be more to the story.

I searched through some of the other entries and my stomach folded into knots. They were together a *lot*.

November 15th

I'm trying to keep my composure, but some days it's hard. I should've gone to my dad and told him what was going on in the first place. He would've known what to do. There are some powerful people in his circle of friends. It's too late though.

I had to give in again today. He went down on me and told me he wasn't going to stop until I came. I could see it in his eyes, he would've kept me there for hours if he had to. I had no choice but to fake it. I took two showers tonight and I still feel dirty.

After that entry, they had their meetings in that secret room at the school about two times a week. I had no clue what kind of room it was, but apparently, no one ever used it.

December 28th

The necklace Adam got me is GONE! I left it on my dresser and it's fucking gone. There's no one at home to take it. My parents are away for a weekend at the Biltmore House and my brother's in Colorado with his friend's family. I don't know what to do. How could it have gone missing? Adam's going to be heartbroken when I tell him.

It wouldn't surprise me if Nathan didn't break in and steal it. With her family gone at the time, she was vulnerable. I wondered if he still had it. With evidence like that, they would have an easier time convicting him. I wanted to call Preston and tell him, but I'd left my phone at Glenn's house.

February 14th

I used to love Valentine's Day, but not anymore. Nathan sent me flowers and so did Adam. The card on Nathan's said they were from a secret admirer. My parents thought it was cute. If they only knew the whole story.

Mine and Nathan's secret spot at school has just been claimed by the principal for another office. I'm sure you can imagine my relief. Now there's nowhere for us to go. Nathan's pissed. I want to turn him in so bad. There's no telling how many students he's tried to blackmail into having sex with him.

And there it was. She'd finally mentioned his name. Granted, it didn't have his last name, but at this point, it was clear who he was. Heart racing, I couldn't wait to tell Preston. Only I knew he wouldn't wait for the police. The kind of punishment Nathan deserved could never be delivered by the cops.

July 23rd

I'm counting down the days until I leave for college. I wish I was there now, away from my life here . . . away from Nathan. He's changed over the summer, gotten a little more aggressive in his attempts to be with me. My birth control pills went missing the other day. I'm starting to think I know who's been in my house, taking my things. When I went for a night walk on the beach, he was there waiting for me.

It wasn't like all the other times. He pulled me forcefully into the sand, his hands rough and desperate. I knew then to never wear a dress again. I had made it easy for him. I told him not to, that I wasn't on the pill anymore, but he still came inside me. It was then I realized his plan. He wants me pregnant.

"Holy shit," I whispered, clutching my stomach. It all made me sick. I heard Preston come back in and I couldn't wait to tell him what I'd found. "Hey, you will not *believe* what I just read." Jumping off the bed, I hurried to the door, only to stop dead in my tracks. Standing at the top of the stairs wasn't Preston. "What the hell are you doing here?"

Eyes wide, Nathan stared at me, his chest rising and falling with rapid breaths. "I didn't think it was possible," he murmured. Stepping forward, he was clearly not in his right mind by the look in his eyes.

I was too stunned to do anything, so I moved back. Did he really think I was Cameron? "How did you get in here?" I asked. That's when I looked down, seeing a key in his hand. He'd sealed his fate with this move. All I had to do was keep him occupied until Preston got there. It didn't help that I was scared to death. I wanted to run, but I had to stay calm.

His attention focused on the boxes and his eyes darkened when he looked up at me. "You weren't going to leave without seeing me first, were you?"

I swallowed hard. "Of course not."

"Where's your ring?" he demanded, glaring at my hand. "I want to see it on you. When you go away to school, I want everyone to know you're taken."

Silently, I prayed to God for help. I didn't know how long I was going to be able to play along before I panicked. My fight or flight response was on the verge of kicking in. With shaky hands, I reached for Skittles and opened her pouch to get the ring. He watched me slide it down on my finger.

"It's a beautiful ring," I said, voice cracking. He moved closer and I trembled when he touched my face. I'd never been so afraid in my life.

"What about your boyfriend? Don't you think it's time you broke it off?"

So many scenarios ran through my mind. Was this Cameron's final moment with him? She must've done or said something to make him snap. I didn't want to do that. "Yes," I agreed. "I don't love him anymore. Not like I love you."

Releasing a sigh, he closed the distance and I backed into the wall as his body pressed against mine. "You have no idea how long I've waited to hear those words come from your lips." He kissed me and I gave in, waiting for the chance to run. "I love you, Cameron. For the longest time, I—I thought I'd lost you. I thought . . ." He stopped and squeezed his eyes shut. "But then, here you are," he finished.

His mind was playing tricks on him. There was something totally fucked up in that brain of his. "I'm still here," I said.

His eyes opened. "I came to tell you that once summer's over, I'll be moving to be with you. That way, we can be together, just like we always wanted."

"I can't wait." I tried to move around him, but he grabbed my hips, pushing me toward the bed.

"You have no idea how happy this makes me. Let's celebrate."

Sucking in a breath, I fell backward as he pushed me

onto the bed, and crawled on top of me. Pressing me into the mattress, he grabbed my breasts with bruising force, his arousal pushing into my hip. I tried to scream out, but he slapped a hand to my mouth. "Shush now. You know I don't like it when you scream."

Tears burned my eyes. I could only imagine the vile things Cameron had to endure with him. He moved his hand from my mouth and it gave me the leverage I needed to push him up and away from me. "I'm not ready. I still have to pack."

His eyes blazed with impatience. "You can do it later," he growled, ripping my T-shirt down the front. Next, he tried to restrain my arms, but I jerked out of his hold.

"I said *no*," I screamed, slapping him across the face.

His head snapped to the side and everything changed for the worse. It brought him back to reality. The murderous glare he gave me sent chills up my spine. Boxing me in with his body, he let loose his rage. "I never let *Cameron* get away with that shit," he snarled, gripping my wrists as hard as he could. I cried out as the pain shot up my arms. "Why the fuck do you think I'd let you do it, Emma?" Jerking my arms above my head, he pressed his weight completely on top of me.

I couldn't move or breathe. "I could ask you the same thing," I gasped. "You don't belong here."

He looked at my hand and pulled the ring off my finger. "How do you have this?" When I didn't answer, he slapped me so hard I was sure he'd split my skin open. "Tell me."

The fear I felt earlier turned to rage. I had to fight for

myself, for Cameron. "Cameron wanted it found," I hissed. "That way we'd know who *killed* her!"

For a split second, he appeared stunned. I took that as my opportunity. As hard as I could, I jerked out of his hold and elbowed him across the face. Blood poured out of his nose and he shouted in pain. I was able to slip out from under him, but before I could get to the door, he tackled me into the wall and we toppled to the floor.

"Preston!" I screamed, hoping like hell he could hear my cries through the open window. The impact of the fall made my breath whoosh out of my lungs. Nathan laid on my back, holding my hands together in a tight grip. I gasped for air, then felt the sharp pain on my head as Nathan jerked my head back by the hair, his hot breath on my ear.

"You thought you could fool me? You're nothing but a whore, just like Cameron. She fucked up by choosing her boyfriend over me."

"What about her mother?"

He scoffed. "Collateral damage. The bitch tried to intervene." His weight lifted but then he turned me around, pinning me on my back with his hands holding my wrists.

"You're pathetic," I spat. "How could anyone love a man who has to blackmail them to have sex with them?"

"I wanted her!" he screamed, pressing his body into mine. "And she's not here. But you are, aren't you? My, my . . . how much you remind me of her." He bent down and ravaged my mouth, forcing his way inside.

I wanted to vomit. With a wave of adrenaline, I bit down on his bottom lip, hard—teeth slicing into his skin. Turning my head, I pulled my teeth to the side, tearing part of his lip wide open. Gagging, I spit his blood to the floor. As I gasped for air, he let out a roar of pain and rage.

Without seeing his face, I knew what was coming. Before he could grab my neck, I wound up and punched him as hard as I could under his chin, but it only angered him more. He sat up and let go of my hands, only so he could get a better angle. His hand collided with the left side of my face so hard, my vision dimmed.

Then, the real pain came. His hands found their way to my neck, grabbing and squeezing so hard, he cut off the oxygen to my lungs. I couldn't breathe. Clawing at his arms, I drew as much blood as I could. He wasn't going to get away this time.

PRESTON

The second I heard Emma scream my name, I dropped everything and raced up the front porch stairs. The door was locked, but I burst through with a swift kick and ran up the stairs as fast as I could. Nothing could have prepared me for what I walked in on.

Nathan was on top of Emma, hands at her throat, blood dripping onto her face from his mangled mouth. She was trying to fight him off, but he was too strong.

I lunged at him full force and tackled him to the floor. "You son of a bitch!" Punching him in the jaw, the sound of his bones cracking brought a smile to my face. I hit him again and again. Rage consumed me and all I wanted was his blood. He had to pay for what he did to my mother and sister. To Emma.

I wanted nothing more than to end it all, but I had to make him suffer. It was only fair. Wrapping my hands around his neck, I squeezed. He grabbed at my wrists, his eyes wide and bloodshot. "Do you know who I am?" I demanded.

He closed his eyes, gasping for the little bit of air I was letting through.

I wanted him to feel pain and fear, it couldn't end too soon. "You killed my mother and sister in cold blood, you fucking bastard. Now *you're* going to die." I squeezed harder. "Enjoy hell, cocksucker."

His face turned purple and his grip on my wrists loosened. Letting go, I allowed him one last ragged breath, a last dose of hope, before whispering, "Cameron never loved you," then snapping his neck completely.

I dropped his lifeless body to the floor and hurried over to Emma, who was on her hands and knees, struggling to breathe. Rubbing her back, I pulled out my phone. "I'm here, angel. You're going to be fine."

She cried and rocked back and forth. "Preston."

"Shh, don't talk. I'm calling for help."

Once the call was made and Emma had calmed down enough to get some air into her lungs, I carried her downstairs and sat her down on the couch. Running into the kitchen, I grabbed some towels and wet them, before rushing back to her. The bruises on her neck were already turning dark. I should've made the bastard suffer longer.

Wiping his blood off her face, the sheer weight of the moment hit me and I broke down. "I'm so sorry I wasn't here. This never would've happened if—"

She touched my cheek, her voice raspy. "We never would've gotten him if you were. You did nothing wrong."

I scoffed. "I almost lost you."

"But you got *him*. And I'm still here, baby. It's a win-win."

It wasn't long before sirens blared down the street and officers charged into the house. The paramedics placed Emma on a stretcher. I wanted to go with her, but I knew I had to stay and explain what happened to the cops. Before they could wheel her out, she grabbed my hand, wincing as she tried to talk. I knew it had to hurt.

"Emma, stop. You don't need to talk right now."

"Yes, I do," she whispered hoarsely, pulling on my hand. I moved closer so I could hear. "Get the police to search Nathan's house. He stole things from Cameron as keepsakes. Her necklace." She swallowed again. "His name is in her diary. Look for Valentine's Day."

I kissed her hand. "Thanks, angel. I'll be with you soon." The paramedics looked at me and I nodded for them to take her away.

A few minutes passed and the chief of police walked in. His name was Grady McConnell and he was a good friend of my father and Glenn. He also knew I was part of the FBI. "Preston, it's good to see you again," he said, holding out his hand. "I just wish it was under better circumstances."

I shook his hand. "So do I."

He glanced at the stairs, where two of his men came down. "What's going on?"

"Nathan Cramer's body is upstairs. He's responsible for the deaths of my mother and my sister, and he also tried to kill Emma. I also have reason to believe he's the man who murdered Shelly Price."

His mouth flew open. "Seriously? It was Cramer this whole time?"

I nodded. "Most of the evidence is in my sister's diary. He blackmailed her into having sex with him, while she was still in high school. And he has also recently been following Emma around."

For the next twenty minutes, I went into further detail over the evidence of Nathan's interactions with the people he killed, and the events of our past week.

Grady whistled when I was done. "That is some crazy shit."

"Yeah, tell me about it." I looked at the clock, wondering how Emma was doing, and that reminded me of what she'd said. "Oh, and Emma told me before she was taken away, that Nathan had stolen some of Cameron's things as keepsakes. You need to look for those things when you search his house. The diary should tell you what to look for."

"We will," he said with a nod. "Now go, I've got this covered. I'm sure your dad will want to know what's going on. I'll be in contact first thing in the morning to ask you and Emma some further questions."

"Sounds good." Rushing out to my car, I got in and hurried to the hospital. It was time I gave my father the news.

By the time I got to Emma's room, the doctor was already inside checking her out. Emma smiled when she saw me, which made some of my tension go away. But seeing the bruising on her cheek made the anger come back. The thought of anyone hitting her made my blood boil.

"Other than a bruised neck, cheek, and vocal chords, and a few lacerations on her mouth, she's good to go," the doctor said. "Are you going to be the one taking care of her?"

I nodded. "Yes."

"Okay. She just needs plenty of rest, ice for the neck, and fluids. The sooner the swelling goes down, the sooner her voice will return to normal."

"Thank you, Dr. Wheeler," Emma whispered carefully.

Once the doctor was gone, Emma tried to pick up her shoes and I helped her. "I got it, angel." She sat back down and I slipped her shoes on her feet. "Has anyone called your parents?" I asked.

She shook her head. "I was hoping we wouldn't have to, but once the media finds out, I might not have a choice." Unfortunately, she was right. "Have you told your dad yet?"

"No. I wanted to see you first." Her eyes widened and I held up my hand. "I'm going now, I promise."

"I'll go with you."

"You don't have to, Emma. Bryce is on his way here to take you back to Glenn's." I wanted her there, but I knew she'd already been through too much.

She wrapped her arms around my waist. "I *want* to stay with you. Besides, I'd like to see your dad again."

I didn't have it in me to argue with her. Besides, I wanted her with me, probably more than she wanted me. Knowing I could've lost her terrified the fuck out of me. Holding her hand, we took the elevator to my father's floor. The door to his room was cracked open slightly, and I could hear his labored breathing.

Emma looked up at me and her eyes said it all—he wasn't long for this world.

We walked in and my father's eyes fluttered open. He coughed and a weak smile spread across his face. "My boy," he croaked.

"Hey, Dad." I pulled the chair from the window and placed it next to mine. Gesturing for Emma to sit, I took the seat beside her.

Emma nodded at him. "Hi, David." He turned his head and she smiled sweetly. "It's good to see you again."

His eyes narrowed as he took in her bruised face and neck, then he turned an angry glare my way. I could tell he wanted to blow up, but he didn't have the strength.

With pursed lips, I shook my head. "I didn't hurt her, Dad."

Sucking in a ragged breath, he closed his eyes. "Good. I don't think I could muster the strength to beat your ass."

"I'm sure you could, if you tried."

He opened his eyes and tried his best to smile, then he

glanced over at Emma again. "Who hit you?" he asked her. "Hopefully, my son made them regret it."

Tears fell down her cheeks. "He did more than that. I'm sure he wants to be the one to tell you."

"I got him, Dad," I said, the words catching in my throat. The emotional toll it had taken on us, on our relationship . . . it was all too much to process.

Tears welled in my dad's eyes, his heart rate spiking, sending the machines into a frenzy. He tried to wipe his eyes, but didn't have the strength. When I grabbed a tissue and did it for him, he touched my arm. "Who was it? Tell me everything."

And that was when I sat on the side of his bed and told him every last detail, from beginning to the end. It was as if the weight lifted off my chest when I was done. I felt like a free man. I'd spent years obsessing over my mother and sister's murders. The guilt had plagued me every day of my life.

My father wept. "My baby girl." He shook his head, dealing with the pain of his daughter's loss all over again. When he was all cried out, he looked at me and patted my hand. "You did it. You did what I couldn't do. I've never been more proud."

I reached for his hand and squeezed. "I'm just sorry it took so long."

"No. You made it right on time." His eyes grew tired, but he made an effort to look at me before he closed them. "I love you, son. Thank you."

Emma turned her head and wiped away her tears, but mine fell openly down my face. "I love you too, Dad."

We left his room to let him get some rest and headed home, only to receive a call from his nurse later that night, informing me that he'd passed in his sleep.

34

EMMA

The past three days had been a complete whirlwind. The funeral for Preston's dad happened the day before, with just a small gathering of his closest friends, mainly those in the FBI, including Glenn. Even though it was hard on Preston, he pushed through it. We barely had time to rest with all the media attention. He hated having to be in the spotlight, but solving the Hale case was huge, especially since he was part of the family.

A knock sounded on my door before it opened. I didn't have to look to know who it was.

"Angel, you coming back downstairs?" Walking up behind me, Preston wrapped his arms around my waist.

I leaned back against his chest, loving the way he made me feel safe. "I am," I replied with a sigh. "I just needed a break. We've barely had time to breathe. My parents like you though.

They can't seem to stop talking to you." They'd come as soon as they'd heard, and hadn't left my side since.

His breath tickled my neck when he chuckled. "That's a good thing." He kissed me and I shivered. "But break time's over, baby. Grady's here. He wants to see us."

We'd been waiting to hear what the police found at Nathan's house. I was more than curious. "All right, let's go."

Once downstairs, I waved at my parents, who were busy talking to Mrs. Walker and her husband. Preston took my hand and led me down the hallway to Glenn's office. Glenn leaned against his desk with his arms crossed, his focus on Grady, who sat in a chair across from him with a folder in his hands. When we walked in, they both looked at us and smiled.

Grady stood and held out his hand. "Emma, it's good to see you again."

I shook his hand. "Same to you."

Glenn glanced back and forth, from me to Preston. "Cramer's house has been thoroughly searched. Grady is here to tell us what they found."

All eyes turned to the chief of police. He handed the file to Glenn and when he opened it, there were some photos, but I couldn't tell what they were of. "We found Cameron's necklace and a few other items that belonged to her in Nathan's house. We also found a picture and a bracelet belonging to Shelly Price."

Deep down, we'd known he was the culprit, but it was nice to get proof. Her family would get the answers they needed. I celebrated the victory in my head, then focused back on what Grady was saying.

"Nathan's uncle was tracked down in Columbia, and questioned. He had borrowed Nathan's truck so he could pick up a living room set." That explained why we thought Nathan was in Columbia. "He was informed of his nephew's death, and he wasn't at all surprised."

Brows furrowed, I looked at Preston, who seemed just as confused as me.

"Why is that?" Preston asked.

Grady nodded at the file. "Apparently, Nathan Cramer had a history of mental illness, with violent mood swings. He took medicine for it, but pills can't fix everything."

I scoffed. "How was he even able to work in the school system? Don't they do background checks?"

"They do," Grady said. "That's where Nathan's parents come into the picture. They paid a hefty amount of money to keep their son's medical history a secret. Right now, they're under further investigation. However, we were able to dig up a juvenile police record for Cramer."

I rubbed my neck where it was still bruised. "Probably for stalking."

"Actually, you're close," Grady agreed. "When Nathan was in high school, he got in trouble for peeping in his neighbor's window. She also went to his high school. Her parents let the first incident go, but then he did it again, and *that* family pressed charges. Eventually, Nathan and his parents moved out of state, so he could attend a different school."

Glenn passed me the photos of what the police found, including the necklace Adam gave to Cameron. It was absolutely beautiful. There were other things too, like a monogrammed hairbrush, a bra, and some pictures.

"Are you going to keep Cameron's things for evidence?" Preston asked, his voice low.

Grady nodded. "For now. I'll give them to you once we're done. But do any of you have any questions before I go? I don't want to keep you from your guests."

Glenn lifted his brows at me and I shook my head. Preston held out his hand to the chief. "We're good. Thank you for stopping by."

Grady smiled. "I'll be in touch soon."

Once he left, Glenn patted Preston's shoulder before leaving the room. I started to follow him out, but Preston grabbed my hand. "Not yet, angel. There's something we need to talk about."

I didn't like the way he said it. My stomach clenched and I faced him, not liking the forlorn expression on his face. "What's wrong?"

Clasping my hands, he looked down at them and sighed. "I'm not going back to Charlotte with you tomorrow."

"What?" I gasped, feeling an ache in my chest.

He grabbed my face, his gray eyes full of love. "Sorry, I shouldn't have said it like that." He took a deep breath and let it out slow. "I decided last night to sell my family's house."

"Oh," I said, breathing a sigh of relief. "I can stay and help you move everything out. I'm sure Glenn won't mind."

He shook his head. "That's what I wanted to talk to you about." His hands slid away from my face and my chest tightened as he leaned against Glenn's desk.

"So you *don't* want me to help?"

He stared at me, his gray eyes searching mine. "I think it's something I need to do on my own. I haven't been able to truly face my demons. I need to know I can do it without you."

Lips trembling, emotions raw, I turned my head. "Are you ending things with me?" I knew I was probably being dramatic, and I didn't want to cry in front of him.

"No," he growled, pulling me to him. "That's never going to happen." Grabbing my chin, he made me look at him. "I love you, Emma. It's going to kill me watching you leave tomorrow. This whole time I've had *you* to keep me strong. *I* need to know I can do it on my own. Please tell me you understand."

The treacherous tears fell down my cheeks. "I do, but I don't want to leave you. How long will you be gone?"

He shrugged. "Not sure. Just promise me you'll be there when I'm done." His lips closed over mine and he breathed me in. "I've waited my whole life for you, angel. I'm not about to lose you now."

"Then promise you'll find your way back to me."

He kissed me again. "Promise."

EMMA

(Two Weeks Later)

"Are you sure you want to go home?" my mother asked, holding out my purse. She gave me those puppy dog eyes that always worked on my dad.

Chuckling, I took my purse and hugged her. "Yes. I've stayed here the past two weeks. Don't get me wrong, being waited on is nice, but I'm ready to get back to *my* place." Ever since I'd gotten back, my parents wanted me to stay with them so I wouldn't be alone. It was nice at first, but I missed having my own space.

"Fine," she replied, sounding defeated. "Just know you can come back if you don't feel comfortable being alone."

I kissed her cheek and opened the front door. It was time for work. "I love you, Mom. I'll call you when I get off." Hurrying out the door, I got in my car and headed toward downtown.

Preston and I talked every day, and he sounded better each time. I had to believe he'd be coming home soon. Unfortunately, he hadn't said anything about it, but I promised myself I wouldn't push him. I missed him so much.

When I pulled up at work, I parked and headed into the office. About a week ago, Glenn had turned me over to Wade. I was nervous working for him, but I'd been the same way when I started with Glenn. So far, I hadn't messed anything up.

The elevator doors opened and I stepped into the lobby of Chandler Enterprises. John was there, sitting with the new guy Glenn had hired to help with the music department. His name was Martin Ashby, a guy not much older than me, with whitish-blond hair and bright blue eyes. Just by the way he carried himself, I could tell he was a man who knew what he was doing.

A part of me was upset, maybe even a little jealous that Glenn hadn't asked me to take the job, since it was mine and Preston's in the beginning. It made me wonder if Preston had any intention of coming back soon. If he was, why did Glenn hire someone? It wasn't something I wanted to think about.

John looked over and watched me walk off the elevator. "Good morning, beautiful."

I put on a smile and waved at them both. "Good morning, guys. Ready for your first professional gig this weekend?" I asked John.

Martin slapped John on the shoulder. "Of course he

is." Then he winked at me. "You and your partner chose an amazing band."

"Thanks."

John's band wasn't the highlight of the big concert this weekend, but they were the opening act before the main event. They had to start somewhere. Soon, they'd be the main attraction.

John motioned me over, and since I had a few minutes to spare, I joined him and Martin. "You should come out to lunch with us today," he suggested. "I'm working on a new song and I thought you could give me your opinion?"

Just thinking about music made everything better. "Of course. Let me see what's on Mr. Chandler's schedule and I'll get back to you."

"Sounds good."

"Emma?"

I looked over to see Mrs. Marshall, receptionist for Chandler Enterprises, waving me over to her desk. She was in her early sixties and had worked for Glenn since he started the company.

By the time I got to her desk, she'd just hung up the phone. "Good morning, Mrs. Marshall."

She always wore bright colors, and she didn't disappoint today in her yellow blouse and white skirt. It went perfect with her bubbly personality. "Good morning, honey. I just got off the phone with Mr. Chandler. He wants to see you in his office."

Glenn was out of town, so it was Wade who needed me.

"Thanks. I'll head there now." Now that I didn't work for Glenn, my office had been switched to the opposite side of the building to put me closer to Wade. I couldn't complain, it had one of the best views of downtown Charlotte.

Wade's door was closed, so I knocked.

"Come in," he called out. I opened the door and smiled as he looked up from the stack of paperwork and nodded at the seat across from him. "Have a seat, Emma."

I sat down and he leaned back in his chair, his expression serious. He had a tendency to lean to the serious side of things, always dressed in his crisp suits. And unfortunately, it didn't look like he had good news.

Palms sweaty, I bit my lip, waiting for him to speak. I was afraid it was going to be about Preston. "Is something wrong?" I asked, breaking the silence.

His brows furrowed. "Why would something be wrong?"

I shrugged. "I don't know. You look like you're about to tell me something I don't want to hear."

Sighing, he leaned forward and clasped his hands on the desk. "I'm sorry, Emma. I brought you in here because I'm letting you go."

My breath hitched and I froze. Had I heard him right? "Excuse me? What do you mean?"

He looked right into my eyes. "You're fired, Emma. You're no longer my assistant."

The blood rushed from my face and I'd probably turned all shades of white. I felt like I was going to throw up. "Fired? I don't understand. Did I do something wrong?"

"Yes, you did," a voice said from behind.

Gasping, I jumped out of the seat and turned around. Could it really be him?

There, standing in the doorway, was Preston, dressed in a pair of khaki shorts and a T-shirt, with the biggest grin on his face. He held out his arms and I ran into them. As soon as I felt his arms wrap around me, I burst into tears.

"You're back," I cried, breathing him in, thankful it wasn't just a dream.

He chuckled. "That I am, angel. And I'm not going anywhere this time."

I let him go and wiped my eyes, while Wade stood with a smirk on his face and came over to shake Preston's hand. "It's good to have you back, brother."

"Happy to be here," Preston replied, releasing his hand.

"What's going on?" I asked, clearly confused.

Preston grinned. "Do you want to know why Wade fired you?" When I shook my head, he pulled me into his arms again. "You were working for the wrong man."

"I don't understand," I said, glancing at them both.

Wade patted Preston's shoulder and walked back over to his desk. "I'm letting you go, so you can work with Preston. You're being transferred over to the music department, effective today."

"What about my office? Do I need to move everything out?" I'd just moved everything in there.

He shook his head. "It's all yours. Now, if you'll excuse me, I have a meeting. I'm sure you two want to catch up. Just, keep it PG-13 . . . and nowhere near my desk."

As soon as he left, I jumped and wrapped my arms around Preston's neck. "I can't believe you're back. I wanted to ask you so many times when I was going to see you again."

He kissed me and I never wanted it to end. "You have no idea how much I missed you. There was a lot to take care of with my father's passing. I didn't want you having to deal with all of the paperwork bullshit."

I pressed a finger to his lips. "You don't have to explain. You're back. That's all that matters."

His arms tightened around my waist. "And now that I'm here, does the offer still stand on staying at your place? Or do I need to go house hunting?"

"Definitely not. You're staying with me. We have to make up for lost time, and that could take weeks, maybe even months."

His hands slid lower down my back. "I can live with that. However, there is something we need to discuss."

"Go on," I told him.

"There might be nights I don't come home right away." The dark look in his gray gaze told me everything I needed to know. "I want you to understand . . ."

I shook my head and silenced him with a kiss. "I understand. You don't have to explain. I'm not going to stop you from righting wrongs."

He caressed my cheek. "Do you have any idea how much I love you?"

I winked. "Probably not as much as I love you."

Lips pursed, his gaze narrowed at me. "Doubtful. Although, we do have a problem."

"What?"

"Did I hear you're going to lunch with John and the other guys? I leave for two weeks and you're already making dates with other men?"

Giggling, I rolled my eyes. "It's not like that. He wants me to look over the song he's writing."

"Good. I'm joining you."

"I don't think you were invited," I teased.

"As one of his managers, I am. It's part of what we'll be doing. John and his band are going to be our first clients. You and I will be working one on one with them."

"Really?" I shrieked excitedly. It was going to feel amazing to be around music again.

Preston nodded. "Glenn's been setting this up all week."

"And you knew?" His smile grew wider. "You're such an ass," I growled, smacking his arm. "I can't believe you didn't tell me."

"Glenn and I wanted it to be a surprise."

"Then why did he hire Martin?"

Preston bit his lip and his face brightened. "Martin's going to start working with another group, toward the end of the year. That is, if they can get all of their bandmates on board. In the meantime, he's going to scout for other talent."

"What group?" I asked. But when all he did was smile and raise his eyebrows, my heart stopped. Could it really be happening? I squeezed his arms and felt my whole body shake. "You can't be serious."

"I am, angel. We owe it to ourselves to try. If we fail, then so be it."

Squealing with delight, I jumped on him and kissed his face. "We won't fail. I can promise you that."

36

EMMA

(Four Months Later)

"I can't believe there's so much snow." We were almost to the end of our road trip to Cliff and Andrea's house, and everywhere you looked was covered in white. There were piles of snow on the sides of the road.

Preston chuckled. "It's December in Maine, Emma."

"It's a good thing I bought some winter clothes." Living in North Carolina, there was never much snow. I barely even wore a coat in the winter. It was going to be nice having a white Christmas for once.

"Did you text Andrea and tell her we're almost there?"

"I did. They're so excited to see you. I can't wait to tell Cliff the news." We wanted to tell them face to face about the possibility of our band reuniting. With them about to have a baby, we didn't know if it'd be possible. Either way, I was excited to see my friends.

Pulling into their driveway, I squealed when I saw their house. They had Christmas lights up and red ribbons draped on their porch. Add in the snow and it was absolutely breathtaking.

"I'm so glad we decided to spend Christmas here," I gushed.

Preston parked the car and smiled. "And you're sure your parents aren't mad we're spending Christmas here and not with them?"

I shook my head. "I told them we'll see them when we get back. They know we've been dying to take this trip." The door to the house opened and Andrea appeared, her belly so big, she looked like she was about to pop. She was still as beautiful as ever, with her dark chocolate hair and creamy skin. "There she is," I squealed, jumping out of the car.

Andrea flung open the screen door and waved. "You're here!"

Cliff bounced out of the house and scooped me up before I could get to her. "Don't tell me you were going to hug *her* first? Come on, I've known you longer."

Giggling, I hugged him tight. "Of course not. Let me take a look at you."

He set me down and held out his arms. His dirty blond hair was shaggy under his hat, and instead of a clean-shaven face, he had a beard. "I still look the same, Em."

I rolled my eyes. "Just a little harrier now."

Chuckling, he pushed me toward the door so he could get to Preston. "What's up, man?" he said, hugging Preston tight. Judging by the wide grin on Preston's face, they were going to be just fine.

Andrea waddled down the steps and had tears in her eyes. "It's so good to see you." We hugged and I didn't want to let her go. "I've missed you so much."

"I've missed you too," I cried.

She pulled back and wiped away her tears. "You have no idea how bad I wanted to visit you after that whole ordeal with that psycho."

I shook my head. "It's okay. The doctor forbade it. And by the looks of you, he was right." I giggled. "I'm sorry it took so long to get up here. Preston and I have been super busy with work."

"I heard. Cliff tells me everything about it. I can't imagine how exciting it is to be in the music industry. Your boss is amazing."

"That he is." And she was about to find out how awesome he really was.

Andrea grabbed my arm and pulled me toward the door. "It's cold. Let's go inside. I made you some hot chocolate."

I sighed. "Oh, how much I love you right now." We walked inside to the kitchen and the guys followed behind us. The house smelled wonderful. There were pies on the counter and a ham in the oven. Andrea handed me a cup full of hot chocolate and whipped cream. I took a sip and moaned; it tasted so good. "Thank you. This is absolute heaven."

Cliff took off his hat and ran a hand through his hair. "I hope you guys are hungry. Andrea's been baking for the past three days."

My stomach growled. "Can't wait. But shouldn't you be resting?" I glared at Andrea.

She rolled her eyes. "Just because I'm overdue, it isn't going to keep me from Christmas baking. It's my favorite time of year." The doctors were planning on inducing her in the next couple of days. I wanted to spend time with her before the baby arrived.

"Hopefully, it'll be one of your most memorable ones as well . . . and I'm not just talking about the baby."

Her eyes widened and she gasped. "Oh my God, are you pregnant too?"

I burst out laughing. "No." Then I looked up at Preston and nodded. "Why don't *you* tell them?"

Preston put his arm around my shoulders. "As you know, our boss put us in charge of the music department at Chandler Enterprises. With that being said, he's opened a lot of doors. Not just with our clients, but with . . . *us*."

Cliff's mouth dropped open, but he didn't speak.

Andrea slapped a hand to her mouth. "What are you saying?" she asked, her voice quivering.

Preston walked over to Cliff. "We're saying that Silent Break might make a comeback. That is, if you're interested."

Cliff stood frozen in shock, while Andrea squealed so

loud I had to cover my ears. "Oh my God, this is insane." She grabbed my arm and shook me. "When you told me Preston was back, I knew you should all play again. I can't believe this is happening!"

"What do you say, Cliff? This could be a life changer," I said.

He ran a hand over his face and laughed. "No shit, but I'm totally in. I've waited forever for this."

Preston slapped his shoulder, and then took my hand, his thumb grazing over the engagement ring he'd slipped on my finger a few weeks ago. "So have we, bud. So have we."

THE END

~ Coming April 2017 – Wade's story ~
TARGET (A Circle of Justice Novel)

ABOUT THE AUTHOR

New York Times and *USA Today* bestselling author L. P. Dover is a southern belle living in North Carolina with her husband and two beautiful girls. Before she began her literary journey she worked in periodontics, enjoying the wonderment of dental surgeries.

She loves to write, but she also loves to play tennis, go on mountain hikes and white water rafting, and has a passion for singing. Her two youngest fans expect a concert each and every night before bedtime, usually Christmas carols.

Dover has written countless novels, including her Forever Fae series, the Second Chances series, the Gloves Off series, the Armed & Dangerous series, the Royal Shifters series, and her standalone novel *Love, Lies, and Deception*. Her favorite genre to read and write is romantic suspense, but if she got to choose a setting in which to live, it would be with her faeries in the Land of the Fae.

L.P. Dover is represented by Marisa Corvisiero of Corvisiero Literary Agency and Italia Gandolfo of Gandolfo Helin & Fountain Literary Management for dramatic rights.

Other Titles by
LP DOVER:

FOREVER FAE SERIES

Forever Fae

Betrayals of Spring

Summer of Frost

Reign of Ice

SECOND CHANCES SERIES

Love's Second Chance

Trusting You

Meant for Me

Fighting for Me

Intercepting Love

Catching Summer

Defending Hayden

Last Chance

Intended for Bristol

GLOVES OFF SERIES

A Fighter's Desire: Part One

A Fighter's Desire: Part Two

Tyler's Undoing

Ryley's Revenge

Winter Kiss: Ryley & Ashley [A Gloves Off Novella]

Paxton's Promise

Camden's Redemption

Kyle's Return

ARMED & DANGEROUS SERIES

No Limit

Roped In

High-Sided

Hidden Betrayals (2017)

SOCIETY X SERIES

Dark Room

Viewing Room

Play Room

R0YAL SHIFTERS SERIES

Turn of the Moon

Resisting the Moon

STANDALONE TITLE

Love, Lies, and Deception

Keep reading for an exclusive cover reveal and a sneak peek at No Limit (An Armed & Dangerous Novel) by L.P. Dover.

Title: TARGET

Series: Circle of Justice

Genre: Romantic Suspense

Release Date: April 3, 2017

Blurb:

An assassin . . . that's what I am.

I'm Wade Chandler by day and a killer at night. I get the job done no matter the cost. Not only do I hunt people for the FBI, but I'm also the owner of Chandler Enterprises, one of the top companies in the southeast.

When Brina Carmichael – daughter of the former president – wants my business advice, it's hard to resist her long legs and seductive smile. One thing leads to another and now I'm in too deep.

I can't let her know what I am, but I've never wanted a woman the way I want her.

However, harboring secrets comes at a price and I have a feeling she's keeping some of her own. Especially, when my next mission leads me straight to her. Turns out she's not who I thought she was.

NO
LIMIT

An ARMED AND DANGEROUS novel

L.P. DOVER

PROLOGUE
JASON

"You found me."

If there was ever a moment when I needed to keep my wits about me, it was now. But how could I do that when I wanted nothing more than to snap the man's neck in front of me; to make him bleed like he did the families he murdered.

"Did you think I wouldn't?" I spat through clenched teeth. His file flashed through my mind, the pictures of the carnage he left behind . . . those children. My blood boiled.

He was poised, ready to fight to the death by the look in his eyes. "I guess it was only a matter of time."

His name was Michael Bruxton, a computer analyst with skills matching my own. But he had a sick hobby that cost the lives of three families over the past two weeks. I spent day and night searching for him, and now I found the bastard.

We circled each other in the rundown, abandoned

warehouse he'd holed up in while on the run. On the floor were tokens he stole from his victims. The baby doll with a bright pink dress caught my attention first. My whole body shook with rage. "How could you do it, you sick fuck?"

His eyes sparkled. "It's like putting paint to canvas." He looked down at the things he collected and smiled. "Their pleas for help were music to my ears."

Flashes of the children laying in their own blood, their lives taken from them at such a young age plagued my mind. They were innocent, along with their parents who only wanted to protect them. A man like him deserved to die a slow, painful death . . . and I was going to make sure that happened.

Lunging for him, we went down to the dirty floor, his head slamming against the concrete. He tried to punch me and missed. I couldn't hear anything other than the blood rushing through my veins. Pinning him with my weight, I punched him over and over, the feel of his bones crunching beneath my fist. I didn't know the families who were killed, but I fought for them, bringing their murderer to justice.

The sick fuck spit to clear his throat, blood dribbling down his cheek, and laughed. "I love it when they fight back." He pushed his arousal into me and groaned.

Jesus Christ. Grabbing his neck, I squeezed and snuffed his next words out. "You get off on pain you perverted son of a bitch?" I picked up a brick from nearby and raised it high. "Let's see how you like this." As hard as I could, I slammed it down on his face. "You said screams were music to your ears,"

I yelled into the silence. "Where are the screams now, you bitch?" I slammed the brick back down on his mutilated face over and over again, trying to unsee the pictures of the flayed bodies he'd left behind.

Throwing the brick across the floor, I got up and surveyed the scene, breathing hard. "Now you can't hurt anyone ever again."

"Got anything new comin' up?" Blake asked, leaning against the doorframe.

Strapping on my holster, I shook my head. After everything that happened with Bruxton, I needed a break. "I hope not. You?"

Jaw tight, he trudged into my office, gray eyes full of turmoil. "Actually, I'm headin' out for good. I just wanted to say goodbye."

"What the hell are you talking about? Are you skipping town or quitting the team?"

Blake Evans and the rest of the guys on our team were the best undercover agents in the country. We'd already lost a couple people, including my sister who decided to move away to California to settle down. We couldn't afford to lose another skilled agent.

A small smile splayed across his face as he sat down. "I'm still going to be a part of the team. This is my life. I'll just be living it somewhere else."

"Where to?"

"Wyoming. My grandfather passed away and left me his ranch. I figured I'd go since nothing's really keeping me here. I'm single, and we're always traveling with the job. I'm never in Charlotte that much anyway."

"No shit. I think this is the first week in months I've been able to sit back and relax." I stared at him and chuckled. "Blake Evans turned cowboy. I never would've thought it."

He got to his feet. "Me neither, but it'll sure be interesting. How about we get one last drink together at Second Street before I go?"

"Sounds good, bro. I was just about to head out." We got halfway to the door when my cell phone rang. I looked down at my phone and walked back to my desk. "It's the Chief of Police from Vegas." So much for the break I wanted. Leaning against my desk, I answered the call. "Ryan Griffin, to what do I owe the pleasure?"

"No pleasure in this call, son. Are you still at the station?"

"I was just getting ready to leave. What do you need?"

Sounding tired, he sighed. "I sent you some files. Take a look at them for me."

Blake took a seat while I sat back down behind my computer. It didn't take long for it to boot back up and when it did, I found the files. "All right, I have the files opened up." The first one was a woman who was found dead two months prior, followed by two other murder victims and one who was missing. "What the fuck is this?"

"Whoever this fucker is, he's cutting them, strangling them, and then leaving them on the side of the road."

I waved Blake over. "Take a look at this," I whispered, holding the phone away. While he sat down, I moved back. "Did it all start two months ago with this first woman, or have you had similar cases?"

"Nope, all new. We've had eyewitnesses give us descriptions of the people these women were last seen with—all high rollers of Sin City. No one wants to talk. All we're getting are dead ends. I need someone on the inside who doesn't look like a cop. My people can't get close enough."

Blake moved out of the way and I glanced at the pictures one last time before closing them out. "I'll be there soon," I said, hanging up.

"That's some really nasty shit going on out there," Blake stated.

Anger boiled in my veins. The pictures of those women were going to forever be ingrained in my mind. "Yes, it is, and I'm going to make sure I find the fucker responsible."

Made in the USA
Middletown, DE
06 November 2021

51771583R00175